The Engagement

Ola Wegner

CHAPTER ONE

Elizabeth glanced up at the tall man walking beside her, his gait confident and well measured. He was looking straight ahead, seemingly not minding anyone or anything around him. A good few minutes had passed since her confession about her changed feelings for him, and his subsequent reaction had been spoken when he had called her his dearest, loveliest Elizabeth. She could hardly believe the sudden turn of events. Only several days ago she had been in despair, mourning that she had lost Darcy forever, almost certain that she had buried her chance at happiness with a man whom she loved deeply despite her initial prejudice and dislike of him.

"When can I speak with your father?" His sudden question brought her from her thoughts to the present moment. He was looking down at her with those dark brown, serious eyes.

"Tonight?" she asked, unsure. "No, tomorrow would be better. I should first speak to Papa about our understanding, explain everything to him."

Darcy nodded, and they walked silently for a moment longer. It was considerably difficult to move calmly by his side. She wished to run with her hands in the air, crying out her joy to the entire world. Above all, everything inside her craved to touch and embrace him, but she hesitated. The way he looked at her when she had reassured him of her changed feelings for him would have burned ice, but he made no attempt to close the physical space between them. Was it because they were in the middle of the road leading to Meryton, or was he simply reserved by nature?

The wind blew strongly in her face, making her blink against the dirt from the road and the dust from the autumn leaves pinching her eyes.

"The weather is changing," Darcy stated, blocking her way with his body to protect her from the wind.

"Perhaps we should return."

Elizabeth took a step closer to him, looking up. When she did not react to his suggestion, he put his hand on her arm, giving her a questioning gaze. "Elizabeth?"

She stared at his large hand cupping the upper part of the sleeve of her ruddy spencer. He was not wearing his gloves, and for the first time she paid attention to the shape of his fingers. They were long, but not quite as smooth and delicate as hers. There were some calluses visible, and a small scar on the thumb. The nails were clean, short and square. She imagined those strong fingers touching her bare skin one day in the future, and the vision was so powerful that she closed the space between their bodies without a trace of her earlier hesitation. Balancing on the balls of her feet to make herself taller, she wrapped her arms around his neck, burying her fingers in the longer locks at the nape.

Initially his entire body stiffened at her assault of his person. However, Elizabeth was not one to be discouraged easily. Rising to her tiptoes, she put her head on his chest, not quite brave enough to look into his eyes. His surprise did not last long, as soon she felt his hands setting gently on both sides of her waist, keeping her steadily to him.

"We are in open view," he said. "Anyone can see us."

"I do not care," she answered fiercely, meeting his eyes.

Sighing, he brought one of his arms higher, putting it behind her back, while the other hand found his way to her cheek. He lowered his head, but the wide brim of her bonnet obstructed access to her face. He tugged at the bow under her chin with much persistency and impatience until the ribbons loosened up and he could push the offending piece off her head.

Elizabeth did not pay much attention when the bonnet hit the ground, because Darcy's lips were on hers, his hands on her back and side, pressing her to him. All too soon he pulled away, breaking the kiss, his forehead pressed against hers.

"I should not have done it," he spoke, kissing her forehead.

"You should," Elizabeth argued back. Her heart was racing wildly, which she thought to be the result of the presence of his large hand on her ribcage. It was spread widely, his thumb placed just under the spot where her stays ended, the tip of it touching the underside of her breast.

He chuckled quietly before placing a short but sweet kiss on her lips and pulling back from her. Instantly she felt cold and lonely without the presence of his hands on her and his body next to hers. He picked up the bonnet from the ground, made sure that it was clean, all the dirt brushed off from it, then put it back on her head, tying the ribbons in a pretty bow.

"You are quite skilled at this," Elizabeth said, smoothing the ends of the blue ribbons which fell on her chest.

"Years of practise," he answered easily.

Elizabeth lifted her eyebrow questioningly at him, but his expression was calm and innocent. "Oh?" she asked.

"Georgiana despised wearing the bonnet as a child. She always tried to take it off when she thought that no one was looking. Thankfully she grew out of it."

Elizabeth smiled, imagining a much younger Darcy attempting to put the hat on the little girl who tugged at it and refused wearing it.

"Shall we go?" Darcy extended his arm to her. "Bingley and your sister must be wondering where we are."

Elizabeth accepted his arm, and for the next few minutes they walked in silence. To Elizabeth's surprise, it was Darcy who spoke first.

"When you speak with your father, please do not mention to him my involvement with your youngest sister."

"He will learn about it eventually, if not from me then from

Mr. Gardiner," Elizabeth responded. "Papa still thinks that he needs to repay the money to my uncle."

"I will talk with Mr. Gardiner about this matter, as I would prefer your father to stay unaware of my involvement."

"But why?"

He shrugged his broad shoulders. "I do not see any reason why he should learn about it. What happened with Wickham was inevitable; if not your sister, then some other young woman would have become his victim. I only repaired what I consider to be my past mistakes."

"A thought crossed my mind that you helped my sister because of me."

"Naturally, my love for you was a driving force in this case," he admitted openly. "When I saw you crying your eyes over the letter from Jane at the inn in Lambton, all I wanted to do was to take you in my arms, assure you that everything would be well, that I would do everything in my power to help."

"Why did you not do it?"

He seemed genuinely taken aback with her enquiry. "I had no right to do that. You seemed more favourable to my company than ever before. However, you were still not mine. I knew that I had to act. I needed to find Wickham and make him marry Lydia—it was the only matter on my mind at the time."

"And I thought that you could not wait to leave my

company."

Darcy stopped walking, and lifting his palm to her cheek, he whispered, "Never that." His thumb touched her lower lip. "Never that."

Elizabeth felt the blood flowing into her cheeks again, setting her heart racing. She took a step closer to him, staring into his eyes, but within seconds his hand dropped from her face and he moved forward. Disappointment filled her heart. She'd thought that he would kiss her one more time. Again she had to remind herself that they were in the middle of the road in full view of anyone who might be passing by. Darcy was a very proper and restrained man. There surely would be many occasions in the future where he would show his affection for her.

In silence, they approached the path leading directly to the top of Oakham Mount. Jane and Mr. Bingley had to have reached their destination already, as they were nowhere in sight.

Elizabeth began to climb, with Darcy directly behind her. The path was not particularly steep, but it was uneven, with bulging roots and small rocks emerging from the ground. She did her best to look under her feet, but it was not easy to be mindful when all she could concentrate on was the feeling of Darcy's warm, large hand firmly present on the small of her back, guiding her. He might be reserved and proper, but in this subtle gesture he was stating that their relationship was changed. She was his and he was hers, and this new fact made her heart sing with joy and excitement.

The wind was much stronger on the top of the hill. The green ribbons of the bonnet were slapping Elizabeth's face. Darcy walked past her towards Mr. Bingley, who stood farther away.

"Are you well, Lizzy?" Jane asked, coming to stand close to her. "Your colour is high."

"I am well, Jane," Elizabeth answered, turning away from the direction of the blowing wind, hoping to sound calm and reassuring.

"I do hope that Mr. Darcy's company was not too unpleasant for you," Jane said, her voice concerned.

"On the contrary, sister. I have a feeling that Mr. Darcy and I will be very good friends from now on."

Jane sent her an astonished look, but did not manage to say anything, as Mr. Bingley approached them with Darcy close behind him.

"Darcy does not like the clouds approaching from the east," the younger man said. "We should return to Longbourn."

Bingley and Jane went down first. Darcy helped Elizabeth down the path. Even though she was perfectly capable of walking down by herself, she did not refuse the support of his arm as he guided her down.

If Elizabeth hoped for some opportunity for private conversation on their way home, she was met with disappointment. Strong, cold winds made it difficult to carry on conversation, and the gentlemen hurried them, wishing to get the ladies home before the weather became even worse.

***

"You are engaged to whom?" Mr. Bennet exclaimed, staring with wide eyes at his second daughter.

"To Mr. Darcy, Papa," Elizabeth replied, sitting calmly on a chair in the Longbourn library.

"Are you jesting with me, Lizzy?"

"No, Papa. I am engaged to Mr. Darcy. I love him and I will marry him as soon as can be."

Mr. Bennet dropped heavily into his favourite armchair, being quiet for a minute. "You love him? You always claimed to hate him! You spoke many times about your dislike for his person."

"I did once dislike him," she admitted. "However, it has been many months now that I have felt quite differently about him."

"May I know since when exactly?"

"Last April."

"April? When you visited the Collinses?"

"Indeed. We met again at Rosings Park; you must remember that Lady Catherine is Mr. Darcy's aunt. Then, when I travelled with the Gardiners, I met him again. At the time I was ready to admit to myself that I was in love with him."

Mr. Bennet shook his greying head. "It seems that I know nothing about my daughters, even about you, Lizzy."

"I could hardly speak to you about matters of the heart, Papa. What happened between Mr. Darcy and I was so very personal to me that even Jane does not know about everything. She knows that I do not hate him anymore, but she is not aware of my love for him. I plan to tell her everything tonight."

The room became silent. Elizabeth thought that it was the best to allow her father some time to settle with the news before mentioning that Darcy wanted to speak with him tomorrow. She could understand why her father was in such a shock. She had always criticized Darcy in his company, and now all of a sudden she was announcing her engagement to the man.

"Forgive me, Lizzy," Mr. Bennet spoke at last. "But I cannot understand your decision. Are you certain that you know what you are doing? You remember how he said that you were not handsome enough to dance with, how he humiliated you at the ball last year."

Elizabeth let out a long sigh, forcing a smile. "I do remember, Papa. Mr. Darcy and I were both fools, fighting the attraction between us. But he was the first to acknowledge that he loved me. He proposed to me five months ago but I refused back then."

"You refused him!" Mr. Bennet interrupted.

Elizabeth nodded, then continued, "It took me all those months to understand him and myself, to change my feelings. When he asked again earlier today, I did not hesitate even for a moment."

"I see, but Lizzy, are you truly certain? Once you are married to him there would not be a way to go back. Trust me on this, you may be attracted to his good looks and wealth, but he will be someone who you will spend the rest of your life with. Think about it, child. Can you trust him? Will he treat you right? Do you know what kind of man he is?"

"He is the best man I know, Papa. He cannot advertise his charms, perhaps, but he is kind, loyal and honest."

"Very well, Lizzy, if you are certain of your decision, I will not try to prevent it. You are of age, and I do trust your judgement. Your mother will certainly be pleased with such news."

Elizabeth came to stand by her father's side. "Thank you, Papa. He wants to talk with you. I told him that you would see him tomorrow."

"Tomorrow, then." Mr. Bennet brought her hand to his mouth, kissing it. "I hope that he will be worthy of you."

"He is, Papa."

"I would like to know him better, spend some time in his

company."

"Of course, Papa," Elizabeth agreed with a smile.

Upon leaving the library, Elizabeth thought that the announcement of the news to her father went rather well. She had expected at least some reluctance on her father's part. After all, she had always professed to hate Darcy when in the presence of her family.

Elizabeth was much less eager to share the news with Mrs. Bennet. There was no point in touching the subject with her today, certainly not before Darcy's talk with her father. She knew that her mother, after her initial shock, would be delighted with the news of her second daughter becoming Mrs. Darcy of Pemberley. What she did not anticipate was that Mrs. Bennet would surely begin to fawn over Darcy even more than she had done over Wickham and Mr. Bingley. If Elizabeth could keep the news from her mother for a day or two, she would, sparing herself and Darcy a lot of embarrassment.

As for Jane, Elizabeth knew that she could trust her sister's good heart and reasoning. Jane would be surprised at first, but also very happy that Elizabeth found happiness the same as she had.

CHAPTER TWO

Jane stared at her with wide blue eyes, her delicate pink lips open. "You cannot be serious, Lizzy."

Elizabeth laughed quietly at her sister's stunned expression. "It is the truth, Jane. Mr. Darcy and I are engaged. He asked me again and I said yes."

"I cannot believe it, sister. You have always hated him!"

"I disliked him strongly in the past, I cannot deny it. However, my feelings have changed. I truly love him now."

"Be serious, Lizzy," Jane insisted. "For how long have you been loving him?"

Elizabeth bit on her lower lip, trying to suppress her amusement and speak seriously. "It was coming so gradually. I began to alter my opinion the next day after the terrible evening at Hunsford when I read his letter. Then when I saw the beauty of Pemberley, realizing that of all that I could have been mistress, my appreciation for him grew greatly."

Jane laughed. "Do not be silly, Lizzy, it is a serious matter. We both know that you do not care that he is rich."

"But Pemberley is a beautiful place," Elizabeth argued.

"You knew about it before his first proposal and you refused him," Jane insisted. "Tell me now, when did you know that you had feelings for him?"

"Well, I think I knew that I loved him when I thought that I lost him forever. The day he found me reading a letter from you in Lambton's inn. I mentioned it to you before. Aunt and Uncle went to church and he met me alone as I was crying over the news about Lydia. He was polite and caring but also distant, and he left so abruptly. I thought that he was disgusted with the scandal Lydia brought to our family and that I would never see him again. Since that moment I knew that I cared for him."

"And he was in a hurry to rescue Lydia!" Jane added, the colour on her cheeks high.

"Yes, but back then I would have never guessed that."

"When the letter from Aunt Madeline came revealing how Mr. Darcy found Wickham and helped them to arrange Lydia's marriage, my first thought was that he did it for you."

"I must say that such a possibility crossed my mind as well, but I did not dare to hope."

Jane reached to touch her arm. "I am so pleased for you, Lizzy, that you are as happy as I am."

Elizabeth leaned over to hug her sister. They remained silent for a moment before Jane pulled back to speak.

"Can you imagine Mama's reaction to the news? Three daughters married in one year! I can already see her running around the house in excitement."

"I am not particularly eager for Mama to learn about it,"

Elizabeth admitted grimly.

"Why not, Lizzy? She will be delighted for you."

"Yes, Jane, but can you imagine how she will behave towards Darcy?"

"Charles does not mind Mama."

"Yes, but Fitzwilliam is different. He hates to be the object of such attention."

"Oh, Lizzy, I believe that Mr. Darcy is ready to suffer through a lot to be in your company. Even Mama's exuberance."

Elizabeth smiled. "Perhaps."

"Did you speak to Papa?"

"Yes, I did."

"What was his reaction?"

"Complete and utter astonishment, naturally. While you and Mr. Bingley courted for quite a long time, Papa had no suspicion about Fitzwilliam's interest in my person. However, he agreed to talk with him tomorrow, and he also wants to know him better."

"I dare say that your Mr. Darcy will be in no time his favourite son-in-law," Jane observed.

"Why?"

"Because Mr. Darcy seems as studious as Papa is. They attended the same university, I believe."

"They did," Elizabeth confirmed.

"There, you see? They will be able to talk about it."

"I hope that you are right. I wish for Papa to like Fitzwilliam."

"He will, once he sees how happy you are. Your eyes shine like never before, Lizzy."

"And only yesterday I thought that I had lost him forever!" she exclaimed.

"It is already nearly midnight," Jane mentioned, glancing at the clock on the mantelpiece. "I should return to my room. Today's long walk tired me."

"I cannot imagine how I will fall asleep today, Jane."

Jane tightened her shawl around her shoulders and walked to the door. "Try, Lizzy. You will want to look your best for Mr. Darcy."

"Good night, Jane."

"Good night." Jane smiled and left the room, closing the door quietly after herself.

Elizabeth lay back, her wide eyes open, following the shadows on the ceiling. She was tired, but sleep would not come to her easily.

***

"Lizzy, wake up. Lizzy!" she heard like through a fog as someone tugged at her arm.

In protest against such abrupt intrusion into her sleep, Elizabeth buried her head into a pillow, at the same time trying to pull the bed covers higher over herself. She was not successful in her attempt to return to the sweet heaven of her dreams, as the quilt was yanked away from her, cold air hitting her body clad only in a thin nightdress.

Squinting her eyes against the bright sun coming from the open window, she groaned, "What is the matter, Jane?"

"Why are you still in bed?" her elder sister demanded in a voice much more firm and decided than her usual tone.

"I could not fall asleep last night. I finally managed to do so around two in the morning. What time it is?" she asked, and not waiting for the answer, she turned her head to look at the clock over the mantelpiece. "It is only a quarter past eight. I can still sleep some more," she murmured, blindly reaching for the covers.

Her head was about to touch the still-warm pillow when Jane spoke in a clear voice, "Mr. Darcy is downstairs."

Elizabeth sat up instantly. "He is?"

Jane nodded. "He came well before eight, I believe. Papa was already in the library. They have been locked there together for quite some time now."

Elizabeth scrambled from the bed, running to the washstand. "Oh, Jane, will you help me with my hair?" she asked, splashing her face with cold water.

Twenty minutes later, the sisters were descending the staircase together. Elizabeth had her hair arranged in a simple yet elegant style, pinned high on the top of her head. She was also wearing a new dress, which Jane had encouraged her to choose for this morning.

It was rather quiet downstairs, apart from the muted sounds of the pianoforte coming from the back of the house. Mary was already practising. Mrs. Bennet and Kitty were nowhere in sight, probably still in their bedrooms.

Jane and Elizabeth tiptoed to the door leading to the library. They held their breaths, attempting to hear something. Unfortunately, the door was old and solid, and no sounds were coming through.

Suddenly the door opened, Mr. Bennet standing in the doorframe with the taller figure of Darcy right behind him.

"Jane, Elizabeth." He nodded, the corners of his lips lifting in an amused smile.

"Good morning, Papa," Jane found her voice first.

Mr. Bennet walked past his daughters. "It is almost time for breakfast, is it not? Mr. Darcy will not join us, as he has some urgent business in London to attend today."

"May I speak with Miss Elizabeth before I leave?" Darcy asked, his dark, cocoa eyes resting boldly on Elizabeth's form.

"Naturally," Mr. Bennet agreed pleasantly before extending his arm to Jane. "Shall we, my dear? Let us give your sister and her beau some privacy."

As soon as her sister and father disappeared from view,

Elizabeth walked into the library, closing the door.

"You are returning to London today?" Those were her first words, and she could not hide the disappointment from her tone.

Darcy stepped closer to her, looking down at her from his great height. "Good morning to you too, my dearest Elizabeth."

"Good morning," she murmured, still upset about the news of his departure.

"I have a meeting with my solicitor," he explained. "He has some documents for me to revise and sign. Only three days ago I did not plan to return to Hertfordshire anytime soon, but as you already know, my aunt's sudden visit gave me hope to speak with you again. I was still not entirely certain of your reception, and thus I did not cancel the meeting before my unexpected trip to Netherfield two days ago."

"I see," Elizabeth said, much calmed with his explanations.

"I shall be back tomorrow," he assured, his palm coming to rest on her cheek, stroking it gently.

Her heart began to race instantly at his touch, her skin turning pink. All too soon he dropped his hand from her face, putting it around her shoulders, leading them towards the sofa in the far corner of the room. As they sat down, his arm stretched behind her back, his fingers tracing the details on the lace of her sleeve. His attentions filled her with great joy, and she had no intention of discouraging him in his actions.

"You spoke with Papa for quite a long time," she said, catching his eye. He was observing her closely, but seemed distracted, his gaze wandering, moving from her eyes to her hair, and lower to her neck and shoulders. "Jane said that you came quite early in the morning."

His eyes focused on her face. "I did. Your father is an interesting companion."

"What did he say?"

"We talked mainly about Cambridge."

"Why Cambridge?"

"Because we both went to university there."

Elizabeth felt herself growing impatient. "I know where my father read. What did he say about your proposal?"

"We spoke little about that, we mainly talked about Cambridge and how we both joined the same..."

"I do not care about you two comparing college memories," she interrupted him. "Do not tease me, I beg you."

"It was what we talked about," he insisted. "As soon as I came in and he greeted me, he said that, as you seemed adamant to have me, and as he had no control over your decisions, his wish was to know me better if we were to become a family. Then we discussed Cambridge and our literary interests. He was very keen on hearing about the library at Pemberley. He heard that it was one of the finest in the country. I invited him to visit us at the very first opportunity."

Elizabeth leaned back more securely against his solid form, thinking about what she had just heard. She was hardly surprised with her father's behaviour. Mr. Bennet delighted himself in his own originality, and rarely behaved in a predictable way. Nevertheless, she had expected that he would interrogate Darcy a bit more. Most fathers in this situation would question Darcy about his character, likes and dislikes, habits, lifestyle, financial situation and plans for the future, certainly not about his library and what kind of books he enjoyed to read.

"You seem to be deep in thought. May I ask what weighs on your mind?" His arm lowered now to be wrapped loosely around her waist, drawing her a bit closer to him but still leaving some distance between them.

Turning her head, she looked into his kind eyes. "Only that I should have expected such behaviour from Papa. He despises to behave the way most people would."

"He does not oppose to our marriage. In my view he seemed welcoming, if not enthusiastic to the idea."

"You are correct." She nodded. "He said as much yesterday, that I was of age, and the decision was mine. However, I expected him to question you a bit more about your intentions, plans, and your character."

"He gave his consent. That should be of greatest importance

to us, should it not?"

She smiled, placing her head on his shoulder, her arm coming around his neck, her fingers combing gently through the thick curls resting at the nape. For Elizabeth, it felt perfectly natural to be so close to him, but Darcy stiffened visibly, as if he were uncomfortable with such close proximity. Swiftly kissing her forehead, he gently but firmly released himself from her hold and stood up.

"It is time for me to go."

"So soon? Stay for breakfast," she said, rising to her feet as well.

"I have already eaten at Netherfield. Let us say goodbye here," he proposed.

"Very well," she agreed, albeit reluctantly. She would have preferred to walk him out. "Are you riding by yourself?"

"I have a good horse. It will be faster this way."

She frowned, glancing apprehensively out of the window. It was not raining yet, but the day was going to be cloudy and windy. The weather could be particularly unpredictable this time of the year.

As if reading her thoughts, he said, "Do not fret. I shall be well. I have been riding since I was a scrap of a boy."

"Be careful," she pleaded him. The awareness that he was an excellent rider, perhaps the best she knew, did not change the fact that she would worry about him.

His arms closed around her loosely and she trustingly rested her head on his chest. But he was a tall man! As they stood like this, the top of her head barely reached his chin. He was perfectly still for a moment, his cheek pressed to her temple. "I love you, my dearest, loveliest Elizabeth," he assured in a deep, loving voice which sent shivers down her spine. "I shall return tomorrow, and for the next days and weeks you will have me all to yourself."

A thought crossed her mind that once her mother learned about their engagement, she would hardly have him only for herself, but she said nothing, not wishing to spoil the moment.

As soon as she felt him separating from her, she rose on the balls of her feet, and her hands moved up from the place on his chest to wrap around his neck, successfully anchoring him to her so that he could not move away.

His hands settled gently on both sides of her waist, but he did not press her more tightly to himself. All too soon he put her back on her feet, taking a decided step back.

He bowed deeply before taking her hand in his and bringing it to his lips.

"I will see you tomorrow. Stay safe." With those words, he turned on his heel and left the room without as much as a glance in her direction.

Elizabeth sat down on the nearest chair, her high forehead frowned in confusion. He did not kiss her like yesterday. *He acted as if is he could not wait to walk away from you,* was the first thought that crossed her mind. Instantly, she scolded herself for making an observation like that. He was simply a very busy man and in a hurry to deal with his business in order to return to her as soon as possible. He had reassured her about his love. Even if he was somehow reserved, she had to remind herself that it was in his character. Surely once they spent more time alone he would become more familiar and open in her presence.

CHAPTER THREE

The rest of the day dragged for Elizabeth. She was restless and jittery. Many times she told herself that it should be a happy day for her, that at last after many misunderstandings and separations, she and Fitzwilliam had found each other, but it did not help much to improve her frame of mind. She missed him. She wished him back with her not tomorrow but now.

The fact that it began to rain heavily soon after his departure only added to the worsening of her mood. Firstly, she was concerned for Darcy, who refused to take a carriage and was travelling on horseback in such dreary weather conditions. Secondly, she was closed up in a house for the entire day, which never failed to dampen her spirits. Not being able to stand her mother's constant chatter, she excused herself to her bedroom. Curling in a windowsill, she stared at the wet world, tracing the patterns of the raindrops on the glass.

A light knock at the door was followed by the sound of the opening door. Without turning her head, she recognised her eldest sister's footsteps.

"Are you well, Lizzy?" Jane asked, taking a seat on a chair

beside her.

Elizabeth placed her head on her bent knees, managing a smile at her beloved sister. "I am well."

"You do not seem well to me." Jane was unconvinced. "Did you have some misunderstanding with Mr. Darcy?"

"No!" Elizabeth denied vehemently. "Of course not! We have been engaged for one day, Jane. How could we have a misunderstanding?"

"You had several in the course of last year," Jane pointed out gently.

"It is not the case now, I assure you. I only would wish him to be here with me. I did not think that we would be separated again, and so soon."

"He had some urgent business in town which could not be delayed, you told me this yourself."

Elizabeth sighed. "I know, and I understand why he had to go, but I miss him."

"I have not seen Charles today and I do miss him as well. Nevertheless, I can see that there is something else which is bothering you, sister," Jane persisted.

"When he was saying goodbye to me, I had the impression that he was in a hurry to leave me."

Jane shook her head in disapproval. "Lizzy, why are you saying such a thing? I am certain that was not the case. He was in hurry because he had business in town; you must take into consideration that he is a busy man with many responsibilities. He cannot devote all his time to you. He promised to be back tomorrow, did he not?"

"He did."

"Then you see that he wishes to be back with you as soon as possible."

"You are right, Jane, I know that you are," Elizabeth acknowledged. "Only..."

"What, Lizzy?"

"He seemed rather reserved."

"Reserved?"

"When I hugged him, or rather attempted to, he pushed me away from him so quickly."

Jane did not respond for a moment longer, her expression thoughtful. "Mr. Darcy is a very proper gentleman. He might not have felt comfortable to show his affection so openly in Papa's library, especially so early in your betrothal. I am certain that in time he will be less reserved with you." She reached for Elizabeth's hand, patting it reassuringly. "Everyone is different, sister, you have to remember that. I can tell you from my own perspective, although I have been engaged for a few weeks only, that the way a man behaves in private, when you are alone, may be quite different than when you two are in the company of others. Charles was rather shy at the very beginning. However, now he has become more..." Jane blushed prettily, looking for the right word, "more bold. You must be patient with your Mr. Darcy. He is undoubtedly more stoic than you are; as you said, more reserved in his behaviours and reactions, but perhaps it is why he has been drawn to you, because of your liveliness and high spirits."

"You are right as always, Jane. I was being silly agonizing over it since the morning."

"I am afraid that moments of doubts cannot be avoided in cases like this, Lizzy. Love brings much joy, but also occasional grief. We are vulnerable as our hearts and souls are opening to another person who is, after all, a stranger. You must remember how nervous I was when Mr. Bingley returned to Netherfield. I could not believe that he was here for me. I was afraid to hope."

Elizabeth smiled warmly at her sister. Jane had suffered much since the last winter. It had been a turbulent year for both sisters, as well as the entire Bennet family.

"You should inform Mama that you are spoken for."

Elizabeth's expression fell. "I should," she agreed. "I have tried to postpone this moment as long as possible."

"Well, I think that it is high time to tell her that by the end of the year she will have three daughters married."

"By the end of the year?"

"Why, of course. I trust that we will be wedded on the same day, sister."

"Mr. Darcy and I have not talked about the exact date yet."

"I do not see the reason why Mr. Darcy would not want to have a Christmas wedding together with Charles and I. Unless you wish for a longer engagement?"

"No, I certainly do not. Now, however, I should truly go to speak to Mama." With those words, Elizabeth rose to her feet, stretching a little. Mrs. Bennet was about to hear the news which would surely make her the happiest woman in all of England.

***

Her mother's reaction was not quite what Elizabeth had envisioned. As she delivered the news of her betrothal to Mr. Darcy of Pemberley, Mrs. Bennet sat calmly, as if transfixed, not uttering a single word. Elizabeth left her in such a state both relieved and slightly apprehensive of such an unexpected reaction. A good quarter of an hour later, she and Jane heard their mother's hurried run through the house. Mrs. Bennet went to her husband for confirmation, and when Mr. Bennet told her that their second daughter was indeed engaged and soon to be Mrs. Fitzwilliam Darcy, the exclamations of joy were heard throughout the entire house. Elizabeth found herself glad that Darcy was not there to witness this spectacle. Mrs. Bennet was in hysterics for the rest of the day, weeping and laughing interchangeably, as well as muttering to herself over and over again 'ten thousand a year or even more'.

Darcy did not return the next day as he promised. Elizabeth eagerly waited for him on the early afternoon, but to no avail. Her disappointment was great, but her concern for his wellbeing was even greater. Darcy was not a man to break his promises. Something must have happened to delay his return. Most likely his business in town took more time than he had initially planned. She tried not to allow the thought that some accident happened to him. Nevertheless, she was worried about him and had a restless night.

The following day around midday, she felt that no longer could she sit by the window, looking out for him. The weather was much improved, and even though it was not sunny, it was not raining either, and the wind had calmed down. She could safely risk a longer walk. She strolled to the Oakham Mount where she had been with Darcy only two days ago. On her way back, she purposely walked the main road hoping to encounter Darcy, but she had no such luck. Tired and cold after a long walk, with her spirits considerably dampened and her petticoats covered in mud, she walked into the warm house with the intention of going to her bedroom first to change and rest by the warm fire.

"Lizzy, child, where have you been?" Her mother's voice made her stop on the first steps of the staircase.

Turning her head, she answered, "On a walk as usual."

Mrs. Bennet's eyes swept her from the tips of her muddy

boots to the top of her messy head. "You look a fright. Go change yourself this instant. Put on that new green dress and repin your hair. If Mr. Darcy sees you like this, he may very well change his mind about marrying you."

Elizabeth leaned over the railing. "He is here?"

"Naturally that he is here. He has been waiting for you for a good hour now. We have barely stopped him from stepping out to look for you."

Not listening anymore, Elizabeth ran up the stairs, taking two steps at a time. Once in her room, she tore off her bonnet and the coat, and kicked off her shoes. Her mother was right. She could hardly show herself to him in such a state. He had seen her worse before, the day she walked three miles to see Jane at Netherfield, but at the time she had not had a care in the world what he had thought about her and her outer appearance. Now the situation was quite different.

A light knock on the door did not divert her attention from the task at hand, which was the hasty removal of her soiled dress. "Come in," she called, being certain that it was Jane willing to help her.

The door opened, but instead of Jane, a tall male figure entered. Elizabeth gasped quietly, instinctively reaching to pick up her dress, which was now pooled around her feet, in order to cover herself. She had her stays and petticoats on, being as much covered as in any summer or ball dress that he had seen her in before, but it felt wrong to allow him to see her only in her undergarments.

"Forgive me," Darcy murmured, looking away from her, taking a step back.

"Please wait," Elizabeth cried out, not wishing for him to leave. "Do not go. Allow me a moment."

Still keeping his eyes away from her form, he nodded, stepping back inside and closing the door. He stood silently, facing the wall, as Elizabeth hastily cleaned the mess of her strewn clothing and put on a fresh dressing gown. It was light blue and shapeless, covering her from her neck to the tips of her feet.

Smoothing her hair, she cleared her throat. "I am decent."

Darcy turned around, his dark eyes sweeping over her form, before setting on her face. "Miss Jane showed me which bedroom was yours," he explained, still visibly embarrassed. "I knocked."

"I thought that it was Jane, offering to help me."

With slight hesitation, Darcy made his way across the room until he stood directly in front of her. Bowing deeply, he took her hand, lifting it to his lips. Elizabeth had the impulse to wrap her arms around his neck, but she fought it. She remembered his resistance last time when she had attempted it.

"Let us sit down," she proposed. Her hand still in his, she led him to the upholstered bench that stood at the end of her bed, which was the only furniture in her room which could fit them both apart from the bed itself. "I was concerned when you did not return yesterday."

"Some complications arose while in London."

"Your business with the solicitor took a longer time than you predicted?"

"No, it was not the case. The meeting went according to the initial plan. I did not predict, though, Georgiana's reaction to the news of our understanding."

Elizabeth sent him a questioning gaze. She remembered Darcy's sister as a sweet girl, shy but eager to befriend her. She could not imagine that Georgiana's reaction to their union might be disapproving.

"Was she not pleased with the news?" she asked.

"Most pleased, to the degree that she insisted on coming with me, which delayed my departure yesterday."

"Your sister is here?" Elizabeth exclaimed.

"She is at Netherfield with her companion, Mrs. Annesley. I though it to be a sound idea not to bring her here with me today yet, which is why I came alone with Bingley. Georgiana is still rather shy, and I do believe that it is wiser to introduce her gradually into the company. I hope to bring her to Longbourn tomorrow, or perhaps you and Jane could visit her at Netherfield first."

"Georgiana is a lovely young lady," Elizabeth spoke with

sincerity. "I look forward to spending more time with her."

"She is overjoyed to be gaining a sister in you, as well as being introduced to your family. Somehow she finds the idea of a large family consisting of only sisters very appealing."

"What about Wickham? Even though he and Lydia are in Newcastle, not coming back in the nearest future, he is often mentioned here, especially by my mother."

"Georgiana knows about Lydia's elopement and marriage to Wickham. She will never have to suffer being in Wickham's presence again, I promised it to her. However, she cannot pretend that he does not exist."

Elizabeth looked down at her hand, encompassed in Darcy's much larger one. Wickham would always be persona non grata in their home, the same as Lydia. Elizabeth understood it, and had no intention to ask Darcy to change his mind about this matter. Lydia was a married woman with at least some respectability regained only due to Darcy's actions, his sacrifice, and goodness. Their entire family owed Darcy so much.

"I could ask Papa to speak with my mother about it. He could ask her not to mention Wickham in Georgiana's presence."

"Absolutely not," Darcy said firmly. "Georgiana's failed elopement is a forgotten matter, it is in the past. I do not wish for anyone to have even a shadow of a doubt that something like that might have happened in my sister's past. The only people who know about it are Colonel Fitzwilliam, you, and I, and it must remain like this."

Elizabeth did not think it necessary to tell him that Jane was also a person who knew about Georgiana's past history with Wickham. Her eldest sister was the soul of discretion, and she would never betray her knowledge to anyone, even Bingley.

"Let us not speak about Wickham, though," Darcy proposed in a lighter tone. Like once before when they had been alone in Mr. Bennet's library, he put his arm around her, allowing her to lean into his side. "How have you been for the last two days, my love?"

She blushed instantly at the endearment, her insides warming up. "I have waited for you," she explained. "I worried that something bad might have happened to you when you did not arrive yesterday, although Jane kept assuring me that you were surely well and that your business in town took longer than you initially planned. I also spoke with Mama about our understanding." She cringed inwardly, remembering her mother's reaction. She could only hope that Mrs. Bennet would not start murmuring to herself 'ten thousand pounds or more' in Darcy's presence. "She is very happy with the news that I am spoken for."

"I noticed that as soon as I entered the house today," Darcy said. "She barely paid any attention to Bingley. All her focus was concentrated solely on me."

Elizabeth examined his handsome face, searching for impatience or even disgust at her mother's antics, but she found nothing of the sort there. He looked a little pained, but calm, and above all resigned.

"I am sorry that you have to suffer through this. We can hope that in a few days she will settle down with the news enough to leave you in peace."

"Yes, let us hope for this," he said, sounding rather unconvinced.

With a quiet sigh, she closed her eyes and supported her head on his broad shoulder. She felt him kissing her forehead, as well as gathering her closer to him. "I wish that we could spend this evening all alone, only you and me."

"My sentiments exactly," he responded. "I am afraid that we will have to wait several months before it can happen. Bingley mentioned to me earlier today that Miss Jane wished for a double wedding at Christmas time."

"Yes, Jane and I talked about it. What is your view on that?"

"Our wedding in three months' time, together with your sister and Bingley?" he asked, receiving a nod from her. "I must say that I initially had a shorter betrothal in mind, but I can understand that you wish to be married on the same day as Jane."

Impulsively, Elizabeth wrapped her hands around his lean waist, hiding her face into his neck, whispering, "Thank you."

Grunting shortly as if she had hurt him with the force of her embrace, he kissed the top of her head before pulling away from her. "We should go downstairs before someone begins to look for us," he announced. "I will wait for you outside in the corridor."

"Please stay," she insisted. "I only have to change my dress and smooth my hair." His eyes were wide open and alert when she walked to the closet, opened it, and took out the freshly pressed light green dress. Then, when she turned to walk behind the painted screen in the corner of the room, she caught the expression of both relief and slight disappointment crossing his face. He did not expect her to undress right in front of him, did he?

"Will you come to Netherfield tomorrow together with Jane?" he asked as she was finishing her toilette behind the screen. "Georgiana will feel more at ease if she sees Jane and you first before meeting the rest of the family here at Longbourn."

"I think that is a sound idea," Elizabeth agreed, stepping from behind the screen. She hoped that Darcy would appreciate the effort that she had put into her looks. The dress brought out the green in her eyes and slimmed down her figure. The hairstyle was simple, as she had no help from Jane or the maid to make it more elaborate. However, her eyes were shining, and she did not need to put blush on her cheeks, as they were naturally flushed, especially in Darcy's presence.

"You look lovely," Darcy said, rushing to her side.

"Lovely enough to tempt you?" she teased.

He opened his mouth to respond but then closed it, a slight frown marking his forehead. "You overheard," he said slowly. "That night when we first met, you heard what I spoke to Bingley about you."

"I did."

"I hoped..." He swallowed visibly, looking very ill at ease. "I hoped that you had not overheard me, although I guessed that you had, especially when I remember the words of your initial refusal of my suit."

Elizabeth placed her hand on his chest, resting it there with reassurance she hoped that he could hear. "I was only teasing you, Fitzwilliam."

"You must know that for a very long time I have considered you the handsomest woman of my acquaintance," he spoke ardently, with a note of desperation in his voice.

She laughed joyfully, amused by his seriousness. "Let us put it to rest. In many years we will be telling this story of the false first impressions to our grandchildren, laughing at it."

"I cannot laugh at it now, and I doubt that I will even in many years to come," he spoke seriously, tension written all over his features. "Due to my own stupidity and pride I nearly lost you."

Elizabeth began to understand that in their future dealings she would have to be more careful with her teasing, as Darcy did not take certain matters as lightly as she did. It would require some time and patience to make his manner less rigid and austere.

"I am yours, and we shall not be separated. We were both fortunate enough to find our way to each other and put the misunderstandings and prejudice in the past." As she was saying her assurances with their eyes locked, she noticed both his body and expression gradually relaxing.

She sent him a bright smile, and soon he returned it shyly.

"Shall we?" he asked, offering her his arm.

They walked together side by side out of Elizabeth's bedroom, but as the staircase was too narrow to comfortably fit two people, Elizabeth went first, with Darcy stepping beside her. It was most pleasant, as he placed his hand on her back again, and even if it was a small and innocent touch, she enjoyed it very much.

"Mr. Darcy, here you are!" Mrs. Bennet exclaimed as soon as they entered the drawing room. "I have been wondering where you were, but no one could guess where you went."

Darcy looked uncomfortable for a moment, not ready to admit in front of his mother-in-law-to-be that he had been alone with her daughter in her bedroom upstairs. He did not have to explain himself, though, as Mrs. Bennet continued, not waiting for him to speak.

"Oh, I see that you found Lizzy. I apologize to you, Mr. Darcy, that she was not here when you came earlier today. I told her not to go for a walk, to stay and wait for you, but that girl never listens to me."

Elizabeth sat down next to Jane on a sofa while Darcy occupied a chair next to Bingley.

"It is quite all right, madam," Darcy said. "Miss Elizabeth and I both share a mutual love for nature and long walks. I can understand her perfectly in that respect."

Mrs. Bennet gaped at him for a moment, clearly not certain how to answer. At last she spoke, changing the subject, "I hope that you like lamb and white soup, Mr. Darcy. I personally supervised the dinner preparations. Good cuisine is something I take great pride in, and I can assure you that I passed all my talents in that respect on my daughters. Elizabeth is perfectly capable of running a household even as large and great as yours."

"I have never doubted Miss Elizabeth's abilities in that respect, or any other, for that matter," Darcy assured. "However, I am afraid that I will not be able to stay for dinner tonight. I must return to Netherfield soon."

"Return to Netherfield?!" she screeched, making Darcy wince slightly. "Are you of opinion that the cook there is better than ours?"

"I simply promised my sister that we would dine together."

Mrs. Bennet's blue eyes nearly popped out of her face. "Your sister?"

"My sister Georgiana insisted on accompanying me once she learned of my understanding with Elizabeth. She is resting now at Netherfield with her companion."

"Why did you not bring her here today?"

"She was quite tired today after the sudden journey from London. Georgiana is young and shy, not yet out in the company. I feared that meeting so many new people at once might prove taxing for her. That is why I hoped that Miss Bennet and Miss Elizabeth might pay her a visit tomorrow at Netherfield before she is introduced into larger company."

"How old is she?" Mrs. Bennet wished to know.

"Sixteen."

"Sixteen is not that young at all! I am very surprised to hear that she is not yet out. But as you are raising her yourself, I can understand that you did not have proper advice on that matter. My youngest daughter, Lydia, who also turned sixteen not a long time ago, is already married. You must have heard. She is Mrs. George Wickham now. You know Mr. Wickham, I believe; he is from Derbyshire as well."

As Darcy answered nothing, she continued, not deterred by his silence, "They are residing in Newcastle now. However, I am certain that they will come to attend Elizabeth's wedding."

Elizabeth glanced worriedly at Darcy, who sat with a grim face, his hands fisted on his thighs. "I am afraid that will not be possible, madam," he said.

"Oh, I am certain that dear Wickham will be allowed a few days of leave from his duties to celebrate Elizabeth's wedding. You must know that she was quite a favourite of his last autumn and winter. They made a striking couple on the dance floor, and for a short time I even thought that—"

Mrs. Bennet did not finish because Elizabeth interrupted her, exclaiming, "Mama! I beg you to stop this nonsense."

The older woman looked at her, as if not comprehending why she was being scolded by her own daughter. Only after a minute or so the understanding of the possible implication of her words seemed to dawn on her.

"But Elizabeth never treated dear Wickham seriously!" Mrs. Bennet claimed fiercely. "I had no idea at the time that she had set her sights on you, Mr. Darcy. I should have guessed something when she refused her hand to poor Mr. Collins. I must say that I was quite vexed with her back then. I should have trusted her judgement, I admit it now, as she proved to be such a clever girl, and sneaky too. She had never said a word of your interest in her, Mr. Darcy, and she had her eyes on you all that time. If only she had trusted me and confessed her intentions, I would have advised her admirably. In the end, though, everything has turned so very well, would you not agree? My daughters made fabulous matches so far. I could not be happier for them. Three daughters married in a year! Who would have thought that?"

Elizabeth felt herself growing hot from inside, her finger digging into the smooth material of her skirts. It was certainly not the first time she had felt deeply ashamed with her mother's foolishness; however, she had never felt it so acutely as now.

Darcy stood up quite abruptly. "Bingley, it is time to go," he announced.

"So soon, Mr. Darcy?" Mrs. Bennet cried out.

Darcy bowed to her but did not respond to her plea. Then he stepped to Elizabeth, who did not dare to look at him, still too mortified to even glimpse at him.

"Miss Elizabeth," he spoke quietly, offering his hand to her. She looked up at him at last, tears of humiliation and anger brimming in her eyes. She placed her trembling hand in his. "I will see you tomorrow morning at Netherfield. Will ten o'clock be too early?" he asked, kissing her hand.

She shook her head, not trusting her voice to utter a single word.

"We shall be at Netherfield around ten in the morning, Mr. Darcy," Jane spoke in a calm tone, smiling politely at him.

Darcy placed Elizabeth's hand gently at her knee before marching out of the room, not even waiting for Bingley, who was still saying his goodbyes to Jane.

Elizabeth sat silently, fighting the tears coming to her eyes. She would not be surprised if Darcy refused to see her evermore after her mother's performance. And it was only the first evening out of many like those to come. Oh, how would they survive the next three months of their engagement?

CHAPTER FOUR

"Lizzy, do not think about last evening any more, I beg you," Jane said, reaching for her sister's hand, giving it a squeeze. The sisters were in the carriage on their way to Netherfield. "You do not wish for Mr. Darcy to see you sad and forlorn."

"Oh, Jane!" Elizabeth cried out. "How can I smile after Mama's display of rudeness and bad manners? She clearly implied that there was something between Wickham and I. You see yourself how angry Mr. Darcy was, how abruptly he left."

"We have already discussed it, Sister. I doubt that he was very angry…perhaps slightly exasperated?"

"I do not understand how you can be so calm about it. Last evening was utterly humiliating to our entire family. I dread to think that it is what we will have to suffer for the next three months until the wedding. It is unbearable."

"I think that Mama realized her mistake yesterday and that she will not repeat it in the future."

However, Elizabeth was inconsolable that morning. "Only something worse," she insisted.

Jane sighed. "Mama is not perfect. However, she loves us and wishes the best for us. Her intentions are always good. She cannot help that she is less clever when it comes to certain matters."

Elizabeth bit down on her lip, staring stubbornly outside the window. She had never truly felt that their mother loved her in particular. Now she could only think that her mother's actions from yesterday's evening were made out of spite, nothing more.

"We are here," Jane said a moment later, handing her a handkerchief. Elizabeth dried her cheeks quickly where a few tears had fallen down. She hardly looked her best today, as her eyes were swollen after the crying she had in her bedroom during the night.

The carriage stopped and the door opened. Bingley's boyish face appeared, greeting them with a wide smile before handing Jane down first. Elizabeth shifted to the door, expecting to see her sister's betrothed returning to help her as well, but to her joy it was Darcy who appeared.

The gravelled path was wet from the night's rain, and there were sizeable puddles marking the ground. Elizabeth looked down with concern at her elegant shoes, regretting not putting on her trusty, leather walking boots. Darcy's gaze followed hers, and guessing her dilemma, he said, "Allow me." Then he reached to have his arm wrapped around her waist, and carried her from the carriage onto the stone stairs leading to the main door.

"Thank you," she whispered, looking up at him.

His hands were still settled on both sides of her midsection, his eyes warm and loving. Most of the tension she had carried inside of her since last night went away, the sensation of calm enveloping her.

"Come," he said, to her regret stepping away from her but offering his arm. "Georgiana is eagerly awaiting you."

Elizabeth found Darcy's sister just as lovely and shy as the last summer. There was no doubt that she was delighted with her brother's engagement. Elizabeth had feared that Georgiana might see her differently now that Lydia was married to Wickham, but there was nothing in the girl's behaviour or manner which could indicate that. On the contrary, Georgiana was most enthusiastic to befriend not only Elizabeth but also Jane. Moreover, she was open to the idea of visiting Longbourn in the next few days to meet Mary and Kitty. Twice she repeated how unusual and delightful it seemed to her to live in a house with so many sisters so close in age. Elizabeth teased her that it was less delightful on days when there were quarrels over the ownership of the bonnets and ribbons, or when all the sisters were attending the same ball or a party and there was only one maid to help with hair and dressing.

They enjoyed tea, excellent cake and pleasant conversation, then Elizabeth felt Darcy's hand gently clasping her shoulder. "May I speak with you?" he said in a low voice, his breath tingling her skin at the back of her neck.

Elizabeth looked over at Georgiana, who was in deep conversation with Jane, her companion, Mrs. Annesley, watching them with a kind expression.

"Excuse me," she said, putting down her teacup and rising to her feet. She joined Darcy, who stood a few feet afar, but was a little surprised when he put his hand on the small of her back, guiding her to the door. Silently, they stepped outside into a small hall with several doors leading to different rooms.

"I have an important matter to discuss with you," he said as he took her hand in his, pulling her with him.

They entered the library, and Elizabeth noticed at once that it was as empty as nearly a year ago when she had seen it the last time. She wondered whether Mr. Bingley would wish to buy Netherfield now that he was marrying Jane. Elizabeth was not entirely certain if Jane would be happy living so close to their mother. For once she liked the idea that her future spouse was from the far north, his estate situated nearly a hundred and fifty miles away from Longbourn. She certainly would miss Jane and her father, but the separation from Mrs. Bennet was not unpleasant, especially in her current frame of mind when she was still very much upset with her mother.

She heard the sound of the closing door, and she was on her way to examine the few lone books which occupied the solid oak bookshelves when to her utter surprise she felt herself pinned to Darcy's chest and walked back to the nearest wall so that her back was plastered again the green wallpaper.

She tilted her head questionably at him. "Fitzwilliam?" But he pressed himself against her, cupping her cheek and staring intensely into her eyes. At last she understood that he wished to kiss her, and was about to rise on her toes to make it easier for him, but he did not wait for her invitation, bending his head down to capture her lips with his.

This kiss was entirely different than their first and only one on their way to Oakham Mount. He started with a gentle caress, but soon he was tugging insistently on her lower lip, his tongue pushing into her mouth. She opened it, allowing him to deepen the kiss.

Before long, Elizabeth felt herself lacking for air, her head dizzy, and only Darcy's strong arms seemed to hold her upright. He broke the kiss but did not pull back.

"I planned to wait with this," he said against her neck before placing small kisses along her collarbone. "But after what I heard from your mother yesterday..."

"Do not mind her, she talks nonsense," she begged.

He straightened to his full height but did not step away from her. One of his hands was placed on her waist, the other on her shoulder. His eyes bore into hers, and he tugged down at the long sleeve of her dress together with her chemise, revealing a bare shoulder and part of the arm. "You are mine."

She reached her hand to touch his cheek. "I am," she assured, keeping his gaze steadily.

He bent down, kissing her again with double the ardour. His fingers were clasped around her shoulder, stroking her bare skin.

"Fitzwilliam," she gasped into his mouth as his hand moved lower, pressing over her breast.

He rested his forehead against hers. "You cannot imagine how jealous and furious I was when I saw you talking with Wickham in Meryton, smiling at him, welcoming his attention."

Elizabeth tried to concentrate her scattered thoughts to reply coherently. "It was over a year ago," she said, seeking his mouth again.

He kissed her again, but shortly, then with strange abruptness he straightened to his full height and took a step back. Elizabeth, suddenly disposed of his strong arms upholding her, stumbled forward.

"There, there," he said, snaking his arm around her waist and leading them towards the sofa. Her legs felt weak, but with each step she felt that control over her body was returning to her.

He sat her down before stepping away for a moment. Elizabeth placed her hand under her bosom, trying to calm her racing heart. If one kiss had put her in such a state...

"Here, drink this," she heard, seeing half a glass of amber liquid. Without a word of protest she took it and swallowed a considerable amount. Her throat burned instantly and her eyes watered.

"Strong," she croaked, coughing.

He massaged her back. "Drink some more."

Obediently, she took another small sip before decidedly putting the glass away on the side table. "Too strong for me; I have only ever had a glass of wine at dinner."

"It is Pemberley's speciality, gives us a good profit every year," he explained. "Bingley always asks to send a few bottles to him."

"I do not like it."

"I did not think that you would, but you needed it."

Elizabeth leaned against the upholstered back of the sofa, her eyes focused on his handsome face.

He also seemed to be affected by their earlier encounter: his lips were swollen, his hair mussed, and cheeks and tips of ears flushed. "Why did you say that you should have waited?" she asked. "After all, there is nothing improper in what we have done, taking into consideration our understanding."

"I promised myself to keep myself under good behaviour until the wedding, but now my resolution is foregone. I do not know how I will survive these three months without touching you again." With those words, he leaned forward, placing a kiss on her collarbone, on the exposed tops of her breasts, before resting his chin on her shoulder. Her dress was still tugged down on one side.

"I do not mind," she assured him.

"I noticed," he said, his voice both proud and joyful. He kissed her shoulder before pulling back to look into her face again. "Would you consider an elopement?"

She laughed at his jest.

Not deterred with her amusement, he spoke seriously, "Tomorrow morning, meet me at dawn on the road to Meryton, and in three days we will be in Gretna Green, married."

Elizabeth sobered instantly, her eyes widening when she saw the determination in his dark eyes. "Gretna Green?" she asked in disbelief. "You?"

He closed his eyes for a moment, and when he opened them, he said, "Then perhaps you would consider a shorter engagement, six weeks instead of three months."

Elizabeth frowned, not comprehending the sudden shift in him. Yesterday, he was agreeable with the plans of a Christmas wedding together with Jane and Mr. Bingley, now he was talking about elopement, even though she had always thought him to be the last man in the world to consider such a thing, especially after what had happened to Georgiana, and how disgusted he had been upon hearing the news of Lydia's escape. Could the jealousy over Wickham have caused this sudden shift in his behaviour?

"I would prefer to—" she began, but he interrupted her by putting a finger on her lips, pressing lightly. His expression changed, and he seemed more of his usual, controlled self. "I know, to marry on the same day as your most beloved sister."

She nodded. "Yes."

"I should not have kissed you like that," he lamented.

She smiled. "Kiss me more."

He shook his head no, but when she wrapped her arms around his neck, pulling him to her with all her might, he complied.

"You are an excellent student when it comes to breaking my resolutions, madam. Not for the first time and certainly not for the last. Nevertheless, we have been gone quite a while," he said as he smoothed her hair back in place. There was no mirror in the room, and Elizabeth hoped that she did not look a fright. "Let us go before they start looking for us."

Elizabeth followed him obediently, still dazed from their encounter. She would never look at the Netherfield library in the same way as before. To be perfectly truthful with herself, she was most pleased with what had transpired between them today, and she was already eagerly anticipating the next occasion. How fortunate she was to crave her future husband's touch, his kisses and embraces, to desire him. She could not imagine marrying someone whom she disliked in that respect. Her friend Charlotte came to her mind. Poor Charlotte, forced to bear Mr. Collin's company not only during the days but also the nights.

CHAPTER FIVE

The next fortnight was very happy but also tiring for Elizabeth. She saw Darcy every day, and usually they went on long walks, much longer than she was accustomed to. The good weather held; it was cold, but it was not raining, and the days were mostly sunny, if not windy. Elizabeth guessed that such a form of daily activity was aimed at avoiding her mother's presence. Although Mrs. Bennet was able to mostly curb her tongue when she talked to Darcy, he was very reserved with her. He was certainly not like Mr. Bingley, who was always a perfect and patient audience for his future mother-in-law.

Because they were gone so much, and walking all alone for many hours a day, Elizabeth felt that they should spend more time with Georgiana. Darcy, however, rejected the idea, justifying that his sister was having a very pleasant time in the company of Mary and Kitty, guarded by Mrs. Annesley. Elizabeth was astonished how well Georgiana liked her younger sisters. She played the pianoforte with Mary or walked to Meryton with Kitty, appearing to be perfectly at ease with their company.

Darcy craved the alone time with her, that much was

obvious, but despite plenty of opportunities to repeat their activities from the Netherfield library, nothing of the sort happened again. Elizabeth was more than willing, but her betrothed put himself under strict control. He was always close by her side, touching her back, helping her to cross uneven patches of ground, holding her hand from time to time, but no more passionate kisses and embraces occurred. There was also no more talk about elopement or an earlier wedding.

Elizabeth found herself quite frustrated and confused with his somehow reserved behaviour. However, as the days passed, she settled down to the point that the morning in the Netherfield library seemed not much more than a dream to her.

During their walks, Darcy proved to be in excellent health and very durable. He could easily walk farther than she, not to mention much faster due to his long legs. As they were alone, Darcy opened to her about his life, telling her stories from his childhood and the difficult years when he was faced with his parents' deaths. He also spoke about Pemberley, and for the first time in her life Elizabeth witnessed how someone could be so attached to and proud of his ancestral home.

With great enthusiasm he told her about his plans for the winter that they would spend together in Derbyshire. He praised Pemberley's beauty when the park was covered with snow, when the lake was frozen.

Elizabeth was eagerly anticipating her new life up north, although she could hardly image so much snow. Coming from the south of the country, she had witnessed snow for only a few days every winter, and it was merely a light dusting that melted away almost as soon as it appeared. She knew that she would miss Longbourn and her father, but especially Jane. Mr. Bingley seemed quite decided to stay in the neighbourhood, but no decision about buying Netherfield or any other estate in the area had been made. Elizabeth still hoped that in the future, she and Jane would live closer to each other.

One day after an especially long eight-mile walk, Elizabeth retired to her bed as soon as Darcy said goodbye to her before returning to Netherfield. She refused the dinner, having no appetite. Jane, seeing that her sister was unwell, forced some chicken broth into her. Elizabeth fell asleep the moment her head touched the pillow and was amazed when the next day she woke up well after eleven in the morning. Never in her life had she slept that late. All her body ached, and she had a sore throat as well as a runny nose. After taking her necessities she crawled back to bed, not willing to leave it.

Jane crept into the room about midday, and seeing that Elizabeth was awake, she greeted her with great concern, "How are you feeling, Lizzy?"

"I think I will rest today."

Jane touched her forehead with the back of her hand. "You

are warm."

"I am well, Jane. A bit tired, perhaps."

"I can see that." Jane moved the covers higher, then stepped away, returning with a woollen blanket to tuck it around Elizabeth's shoulders and neck. "I will return shortly with your breakfast."

"My throat hurts," Elizabeth revealed. "I do not believe I will be able to eat much."

"You should eat to get better, Lizzy. You must be hungry, you barely ate anything last night."

Elizabeth yawned. "I only want to sleep," she said.

"Sleep, I will be back soon."

Elizabeth closed her eyes, but it seemed only a moment later when Jane returned together with the maid, bringing the tray filled with more chicken broth, as well as some fruit, cake and tea.

Still feeling tired, Elizabeth remained sitting down in bed, her back supported on numerous pillows.

"Oranges, at this time of the year?" she marvelled, putting a piece of sweet fruit into her mouth.

"Mr. Darcy had them delivered for you when he heard that you were unwell."

"He is here?" Elizabeth enquired with more energy.

"He was in the morning."

Under Jane's watchful eye, Elizabeth had an entire bowl of

hot soup, as well as a slice of cake. She refused anything more, burying herself back into the warm covers.

She must have slept quite a long time, because when she woke up the room was dark, and Darcy sat on a chair next to the bed.

"How are you feeling?" he asked, his hand reaching up to her forehead, cupping her face.

"Better," she answered in a raspy voice, sitting up, keeping the sheet to her chest for decency, as her nightgown was quite thin. She tried to ask him how long he had been sitting here with her but her voice failed her, and she began to cough.

"It is my fault that you became sick," he announced, his expression grave.

She was about to protest, but he raised his hand. "Do not try to deny it. Jane told me that you would not have become sick if you had not walked long miles every day in the cold weather. She was entirely correct."

"I shall be well tomorrow," Elizabeth insisted. "I need some time to rest, that is all."

He moved from his chair, taking a seat on the edge of her bed. He carefully put his arms around her. Elizabeth snuggled into his chest, even though she knew that she should tell him to sit away from her so he would not become sick from the close contact with her.

"My selfish actions brought illness on you," he murmured

against her hair.

Elizabeth began to feel impatient with his self-castigating but did not say a word, enjoying his embrace.

"No long walks after you return to health," he said, to her regret moving away from her, sitting back on his chair. "Not until the weather improves."

"We can sit in a park," she proposed.

He shook his head. "It is too cold."

Elizabeth had a different opinion, but she decided it was not a good moment to present it. In a few days they would surely go for a walk together. Darcy would not stand sitting in a drawing room together with Mrs. Bennet for more than one day.

"Would you like me to read to you?" he asked. "I bought some new books. I do not believe that you are familiar with them."

Elizabeth listened to him reading the account of a journey to the East Indies until it was dark. Then Jane returned with tea. Despite Elizabeth's protest, she told Darcy that her sister needed her rest and that it would be best for him to go now and return tomorrow.

As soon as Darcy said his goodbyes, Elizabeth turned on her sister. "You were barely polite to him, Jane," she accused.

"You became sick because of him, Lizzy."

"Nonsense, Jane. Colds are quite common this time of the

year."

"You have not been ill for the last three or four years," Jane argued. "Had he not dragged you around the fields and pastures many hours a day in cold and sometimes rain, you would have been fine."

"He only wished for us to be alone. You very well know that it is difficult to have privacy in this home."

"In a few months you will be married and he will have as much privacy as he could wish for. He risked your health for his own selfish reasons. He should have known better than that."

Elizabeth was silent as she drank her tea. She tried to put herself in Jane's position. If it had been Mr. Bingley who had made her sister sick, she would not have been pleased with him either.

"He regrets it," Elizabeth said.

"Oh, I know that he does," Jane countered. "I made certain of that."

"What did you tell him, exactly?"

"That you might have developed bronchitis or even pneumonia."

"That is absurd!"

"Is it, Lizzy? Were you of a weaker constitution, I do not know how it would end."

Elizabeth could see that Jane was convinced that she was

right, and that Darcy was not her favourite person in the world today.

As the evening came, Elizabeth began to feel much better. She even wished to go downstairs to join the family for dinner, but Jane insisted that she should stay in her room. Nevertheless, she left the bed and had a warm meal with Jane at the small table which usually served as the writing desk.

Mr. Bennet visited her for some time, the same as Mary and Kitty. Even Mrs. Bennet spent a quarter of an hour with her. She talked mostly about Mr. Darcy and how generous he was, having delivered exotic fruit not only for her but also for the entire family once he learned that she was sick. Elizabeth was surprised that she had come at all to see her. She had never been accustomed to tend to any of her daughters when they had been unwell, leaving it to the nursemaids or their housekeeper, Hill. Elizabeth suspected that her mother's unusual behaviour had its source in the fact that she would become Mrs. Darcy of Pemberley in little over two months.

***

Much to Darcy's joy and relief, Elizabeth returned to health within a few days. She was unable to convince him that she felt well enough to resume their long walks, however. They strolled Longbourn's small park, but he refused to go any farther.

After a week of sitting inside Longbourn in the company of Mrs. Bennet and all the girls, Darcy began to escape to the library, spending hours with Mr. Bennet. It did not please Elizabeth because, although he was close, she had no opportunity to talk with him, and they had very little private time.

Mrs. Bennet was engrossed in preparations of the double wedding which was to take place on the last Sunday of December. As she had no opportunity to participate in Lydia's wedding, who had been married hastily and secretly in London, away from family and friends, she wanted to be certain that this time the entire neighbourhood would see how well her two eldest daughters were marrying.

Elizabeth was not particularly interested in the vast preparations, and allowed her mother and Jane to decide. There was only one matter which Elizabeth disagreed with: A trip to London to order dresses, which Mrs. Bennet insisted on and Jane quietly encouraged, seemed unnecessary. Elizabeth thought that the local seamstress that usually sewed most of their dresses would be capable enough to make two wedding gowns for Jane and her. However, Mrs. Bennet was unyielding in that respect, claiming that only in London they could find the right materials and skilled enough seamstress.

A letter was sent to the Gardiners announcing the arrival of Mrs. Bennet together with Jane and Elizabeth in the first days of November. Mrs. Gardiner, known for her elegance and good taste, was to advice her nieces on the appropriate choices.

Apart from the wedding gowns, which in the future might also be used as ball gowns, Elizabeth and Jane were each to receive four new day dresses, as well as matching spencers, hats, gloves, shoes, numerous stockings, petticoats, nightgowns, and shifts.

Both Elizabeth and Jane were well aware that it was much expense to their parents, but when they tried to mention it to their mother, she shushed them down. Mrs. Bennet insisted that they were not beggars, and that how they presented themselves was of the utmost importance. Specifically, she claimed that the servants at Pemberley should not think that Elizabeth was not fit to be their mistress if, while unpacking her trunks, they were filled with old dresses and threadbare petticoats.

Darcy was most pleased when he heard about the trip to London. He wished to show Elizabeth his 'modest townhouse', as he described it. Elizabeth doubted whether they understood the word 'modest' in the same way in this case, but nevertheless she was eager to see it.

October came to an end and Elizabeth and Jane were to spend one of the last days before their journey to London at Netherfield, on the excuse that Jane needed to decide what changes she wanted to introduce in the house.

They arrived at Netherfield quite early in the morning. Both Darcy and Mr. Bingley awaited them in front of the house as usual.

Elizabeth easily guessed that Darcy wished to engage her entire attention from the time she walked through the threshold. She decided, though, that it was a good opportunity to keep Georgiana's company for a longer time than a short conversation. Elizabeth felt that she should do a much better effort at befriending Darcy's sister. So far, however, it had been a challenge, as most of her time was occupied by Darcy himself.

Today, ignoring Darcy's looks and the longing in his eyes, she sat with Georgiana. Mrs. Annesley retired to her room upstairs, while Bingley and Jane were alone, touring the house, looking at the improvements that should be made.

As they drank tea and partook in refreshments, Elizabeth did her best to engage the young girl in conversation. "I did not have the opportunity to ask you, but please tell me if you are enjoying yourself in here."

"Oh, yes, everyone is so very kind to me. I do like spending time at Longbourn with Kitty and Mary."

Elizabeth smiled. "I am glad to hear that. I wish for you and I to spend more time with each other, though. I am sorry that so far I have had so little time for you."

"I do understand that you need to spend time with Brother," Georgiana assured. "He is very happy, and I am so pleased for him. I have never seen him so." The last words she spoke in a lower voice, presumably to prevent Darcy from overhearing her as he sat brooding by the window with a book in his hand.

"And I do hope that no one or nothing upset you during your stay here," Elizabeth said, carefully observing Georgiana's face. "The company in here must differ from what you are accustomed to."

"It does," Georgiana answered honestly. "I never had many friends or a large company around myself. Since I can remember, it has always just been Brother and I. I do not remember my mother, and Papa had been sick since I was a small child, not leaving his rooms much. There were no cousins my age to play with. But here, there is so much to do every day. Kitty always has delightful ideas on how we should spend our time, while Mary is always willing to practise pianoforte together. Mrs. Bennet is very kind as well, always asking whether I am hungry or needing something."

Elizabeth could see that Georgiana was speaking honestly from her heart, and truly believed it. Perhaps what was often tiring and annoying for Elizabeth, making her escape on her long walks, seemed desirable and attractive for Georgiana, who had had a rather lone existence so far. She could also see that, due to her young age, the girl was enamoured with this new, different life in a house always filled with people and activity, not being able to look at it from a more critical point of view.

Elizabeth was glad that Georgiana had taken so well to life at

Longbourn. However, she could guess that before long Georgiana would become tired with the constant chatter and company. It was good then that they would spend the next weeks in London, before returning to Derbyshire after their wedding.

As Georgiana had not mentioned Wickham's name even once, Elizabeth decided not to question her about him. She was certain that Georgiana must have heard about the man during her stay in Hertfordshire. Nevertheless, she did not give the impression of being upset, or having any care about it. Mrs. Bennet happened to mention Lydia and 'dear Wickham' as she referred to him from time to time, but as Georgiana spent her days in the company of Mary and Kitty, she was sure that her younger sisters did not mention Lydia or her husband very often.

Mary and Lydia had never seen eye to eye, being so very different in every aspect that it was difficult to believe that they were indeed sisters. As for Kitty, even though she was closest in age to Lydia, and they had always kept one another's company, there had never been a true bond between them. Lydia had been always very selfish and quite often unkind, ignoring Kitty in public once the officers were around as well as openly boasting to be Mrs. Bennet's favourite and second-beautiful in the family only after Jane. Thus, it was not a surprise to Elizabeth that once Lydia left first for Brighton, and later for Newcastle with Wickham, Kitty did not seem to miss her much and rarely mentioned her in everyday conversation.

Mr. Bennet, who after Lydia's elopement decided that it was high time to exercise more control over Kitty, forbade her from attending any social gatherings this autumn. She could go only if she was in the company of Elizabeth or Jane, and she was not allowed to dance with any young men. But as Georgiana was not out yet in the world, and could not attend any parties or gatherings, Kitty preferred to spend time together with her new sister.

Elizabeth could not wish a better companion for Kitty and Mary than Georgiana. She had noticed that at first her sisters were a little reserved with the newcomer. Mary felt intimidated, as she had heard how accomplished Georgiana was and how well she played the pianoforte, while Kitty was a bit wary, as never in her life had she met such a distinguished and well-dressed young lady.

Georgiana wore mainly white and pale blue and other pastel colours suiting her delicate features, fair skin, pale blonde hair, blue eyes, and most importantly her young age. Her dresses were simple, sometimes even severe in cut, without bows and frills, but the materials were so very fine and the design so fashionable that there was no doubt that they had come straight from one of the best dressmakers in Bond Street.

However, despite their initial caution, Kitty and Mary quickly recognised that Georgiana was sweet and shy, never putting on airs or looking down at them because of her wealth. On the contrary, she seemed to crave their company and feel genuinely honoured when they offered it. When within a few days since Georgiana's arrival it became obvious that she did not mind sharing her music sheets and ribbons, the fast friendship was forged without much delay.

For the rest of the afternoon Georgiana and Elizabeth talked quietly, and later played the pianoforte together, not being disturbed by anyone. Darcy, who was first engrossed in a book, later began writing letters. He was very quiet, which was not unusual for him. Elizabeth, however, wondered whether he was disappointed that on the day when they could spend time alone she chose his sister over him, or perhaps he did not wish to disturb their interaction. Jane and Bingley chose to abandon the company entirely and for many hours. Elizabeth did not mind, as she would have done the same with Darcy if not for Georgiana.

At last, around four in the afternoon, Jane returned with a red face and a beaming Bingley right behind her. Elizabeth looked discreetly at her elder sister, noticing how pleased Jane looked. While Jane was smiling softly, her whole person glowing, Bingley had such a wide smile on his face that it began to look unnatural after a few minutes. Elizabeth noticed how Darcy rolled his eyes at the ridiculous faces that Bingley wore sitting by Jane's side. Elizabeth knew that Darcy had a sense of humour, even though he disliked showing it openly. She was on a mission to change that. Her man needed to laugh more.

As the nights were dark and moonless, Jane and Elizabeth planned to return home before dinner, leaving not later than at five o'clock. Their plans were postponed, as shortly after four it started to rain so heavily that both Bingley and Darcy protested against travelling in such weather. Elizabeth tried to reason with them, saying that it was only four miles of straight and even road, but Darcy especially was adamant, claiming that even a few miles in such conditions were dangerous. When Jane supported him shyly, claiming that Mama would surely agree with Mr. Darcy that they should not take unnecessary risks, Elizabeth had no other choice but to agree.

The whole company spent a very pleasant evening, eating a good dinner and later enjoying Georgiana's music, who with quiet encouragement from Elizabeth agreed to play for everyone.

As the ladies were tired, especially Jane, the company retired upstairs before ten o'clock. Elizabeth was placed in the same room that she had stayed in when she had been nursing Jane. It was difficult not to draw comparisons between the present moment and what had been a year ago. If a fortune teller had told her back then that at the same time next year her eldest sister would be making preparations for a wedding with Mr. Bingley, she would not have been at all astonished. However, she would have laughed at hearing about the possibility of her and Darcy's engagement. She had strongly believed that he hated her, that he had looked at her only to criticize, that he had despised her whole being.

Shaking her head at how surprising life could be, she prepared herself for the night. Georgiana was kind enough to lend both her and Jane nightclothes, including gowns with matching robes and even slippers, all items looking as if they had never been worn before. Elizabeth wondered for a moment how many sets of unworn clothing the young girl had.

It was close to eleven when Elizabeth put the candles down and climbed into a four-poster bed. Sleep could not come to her, though. Usually when she could not fall asleep it was helpful to read a few chapters of a book that was not overly riveting. For a moment she considered going downstairs to the library in order to pick something, but she rejected it quickly, doubting that she would find anything interesting to read there. Moreover, leaving the warm bed was not her priority, especially on such a cold night.

Soon after the clock struck eleven, there was a knock on the door. Without any hesitation, Elizabeth ran to the bed, thinking that it was surely Jane, or perhaps even Georgiana, even though she doubted that the young girl would find the courage to pay such a late-night visit.

CHAPTER SIX

Her face broke into a wide smile when on her doorstep she saw Darcy dressed casually, without his neck cloth and vest, wearing only a shirt and coat.

"Were you sleeping?" he asked quietly.

Shaking her head, she mouthed, "No."

"Put on your robe and slippers."

Without questioning him she did as she was told, returning to him quickly. He took her hand in his, leading her across the corridor towards the staircase.

"Where are we going?" she whispered.

He squeezed her hand but said nothing, putting a finger to his lips. Suddenly they heard the sound of an opening door. Darcy reacted quickly, pulling Elizabeth into a darkened corner behind a tall armoire, hiding her completely from view with his large body.

Elizabeth's eyes widened at what she saw, craning her neck to see past Darcy's arm. Mr. Bingley was leaving her sister's bedchamber. She opened her mouth, a gasp escaping from it, when Darcy covered the lover part of her face with his hand, lifting his finger once again to his lips, silencing her.

Elizabeth watched with fascination as Jane appeared in the

doorway, pulling Mr. Bingley down for a thorough and passionate kiss. It was not a situation that she would ever expect to see her sister in. The exchange between lovers lasted for a moment longer before Mr. Bingley was pulled back inside and the door was closed with a not-so-quiet click.

Darcy stepped away from her. He reclaimed her hand, moving them from their hiding place.

Elizabeth allowed herself to be led downstairs, not minding where they were going. She did not consider herself an overly prudish person. Nevertheless, what she had just witnessed in the darkened corridor astounded her.

It was pitch-dark downstairs, and she could barely recognise which room they were going toward. At last he opened one of the doors, leading her inside. The library was warm and inviting, lit by the buzzing fireplace and a few thick candles.

"What is that?" she asked, pointing to the mantelpiece. There was a brass pot hanging over the fire, and a thick fur was spread in front of it, along with some pillows.

"It is family tradition at Pemberley. We often drink mulled wine on cold winter evenings. It is not winter yet, but I thought that perhaps we could perform this custom tonight."

He helped Elizabeth to settle in front of the fireplace, placing a tartan blanket around her shoulders. "Warm enough?" he asked.

"Very," she assured him, staring at the fire.

Darcy busied himself with pouring the wine from the pot into the tin cups. "Be careful, it is very hot," he said, handing her the cup. Elizabeth had to wrap the ends of the blanket around the cup, as it was so warm that it was almost uncomfortable to hold.

"Delicious," she praised after enjoying a few sips. It tickled her nose and throat, warming her insides. "What is in there?"

"Raisins and a few spices; quite an old recipe, I believe."

They enjoyed their drinks silently for a moment longer, Elizabeth asking for another helping. Darcy drank only one cup, warning her that it was strong wine and that two cups were quite enough for her.

Indeed, after finishing the second cup she experienced some dizziness and excessive warmth inside her body. She abandoned her blanket, feeling much too hot to bother with it. To her utter humiliation, a quiet but still perfectly well-heard burp formed in her throat. She had never behaved so inelegantly in front of any gentleman.

Hearing Darcy's chuckle, she managed to look at him, and when she saw that he was not disgusted with her lack of decorum, but on the contrary visibly amused, she smiled back at him.

"Forgive me," she said, but as soon as the words left her mouth, she hiccupped again.

Darcy moved closer to her, rubbing her back. Within

seconds she felt very sleepy, and gratefully rested her head on his shoulder. He pulled her into his arms, kissing the top of her head. Elizabeth put her hot cheek on his equally warm shirt-clad chest, fighting her eyelids from shutting down as she stared at the fire.

"We should return upstairs," he whispered, kissing the top of her head again.

"Not yet," she protested.

"It is already well past twelve," he pointed out. "You will find it difficult to wake up tomorrow morning."

"Can we not stay here?"

"And freeze to death?" he questioned reasonably. "Soon the fire will be extinguished, and there are no more logs."

Elizabeth sighed, cuddling closely to him. "A few more minutes then?" she asked, allowing herself to close her eyes.

"Wake up, Lizzy, wake up," she heard, seemingly only a second later. "Come, we must go. The fire has nearly died down."

Yawning loudly, she widened her eyes exaggeratedly to keep them open. With Darcy's help she stood to her feet, but as soon as he let go of her she stumbled forward. Darcy sat her down on a chair, murmuring, "There, there. In the future, no more than one glass of wine for you, my dearest."

"I am perfectly fine," she assured, watching as he tidied the area in front of the fireplace, putting away the fur skin and tartan blanket.

"Come," he said, lifting her to her feet again. Elizabeth managed to walk straight to the door, but outside of it she stumbled again.

Darcy picked her up in his arms, marching decidedly towards the stairs. This manly gesture delighted her to such an extent that she began to giggle quite uncontrollably.

"Shush," he scolded her, but when it did not help he bent his head down, capturing her lips with his.

After a kiss which lasted for the entire flight of stairs, she was effectively silenced, contently snuggled in his embrace.

Once they were back inside her room, he sat her on the bed before striding towards the mantelpiece, rousing the fire anew. As it was blazing again, he made his way back to her. "We will see each other at breakfast tomorrow morning. Have a good night."

To her ears, he sounded much too reserved to her liking. Leaning forward, she caught his sleeve, forcing him to sit on her bed. "Stay," she said.

He gave her a long look, shaking his head decidedly. "No."

Wrapping her fingers tightly around his wrist, she clung to his side. "Stay until I fall asleep."

He hung his head down, letting out a suffering sigh. "Get under the covers," he ordered in a gruff tone, at which she squealed in joy, earning herself a scolding glare and reminding her of the old Mr. Darcy. Touching her finger to her lips, she nodded her head in agreement. “Shush, shush,” she ordered herself.

She removed the robe, allowing it to fall to the floor, than she kicked off her slippers and they followed the robe at the heap beside the bed. She crawled under the sheets, pulling them down to invite Darcy in.

He removed his shoes but nothing more. Then he lay down next to her, but staying on top of the covers. “Sleep,” he said, his finger stroking her cheek in a slow motion.

Elizabeth snuggled close, wrapping her arm around his lean midsection. The wine running through her blood made her forget about propriety. It felt right to have him here, and she did not wish to be left alone. Why should he not stay until morning?

“Sleep,” he repeated.

“You will be gone,” she said, fighting to keep her eyelids open.

He pulled the covers higher over her, putting his arm around her, bringing their bodies closer. “I will stay for a while,” he promised.

Elizabeth nodded, allowing herself to drift away. She was the happiest woman in all of England tonight, there was no doubt about it.

Her sleep was deep and strong, but she was forced to wake

up an hour later when the pressure on her bladder became so great that she had to rise to use the chamber pot. Darcy was nowhere in sight, but as the fire in the room was blazing, the barely smoked logs burning strongly, she could only guess that he had gone not a long time ago.

He'd kept his word. He had stayed with her for some time; he had not left as soon as she had fallen asleep.

***

The following morning they met at the breakfast table. Elizabeth felt shy after their late-night rendezvous, blushing furiously as he greeted her. She remembered quite clearly that she had attempted to coerce him into joining her in the bed. She blamed it on the wine he had given her. She would not have been so forward otherwise. Darcy behaved his usual polite, calm, and reserved self. He took the seat next to Elizabeth, but apart from a squeeze of her hand under the table and a few warm glances, he was entirely focused on the food on his plate. He had to be hungry.

From a glance out of the window one could see that the weather had improved greatly over the night, and there was no reason for the Bennet sisters to say at Netherfield any longer, especially when there was still some packing and last-minute preparations to be done before their trip to London. They were needed at home even though they would prefer to stay here with their men.

Elizabeth stole a few glances at Jane. As her sister noticed her longer-than-usual staring, she earned herself a questioning gaze. There was no difference to be seen in Jane's outer appearance; she looked as beautiful, stoic, and angelic as ever.

Yesterday, Elizabeth had given little thought to what she had witnessed in the corridor, being entirely occupied with Darcy. This morning, however, the scene of Jane and Mr. Bingley, kissing while her sister dragged the man back into her bedroom, stood before her eyes anew, not wishing to go away. For certain she was more than surprised with Jane's behaviour, who in her view was the most proper young woman of her acquaintance. She had never imagined Jane would ever behave with such passionate abandon. On the other hand, she and Mr. Bingley were engaged, in love, soon to be married, and certainly were allowed certain liberties when done in private.

The warm and large presence of Darcy's hand on her leg brought her attention back to the present moment.

"You have eaten very little," he said.

Elizabeth looked down at her unfinished eggs then she smiled at him.

He ran his hand up and down her thigh, which made the blood rise in her cheeks again. Standing up, he took her plate and walked away a few steps to the side cabinet to prepare a fresh plate of warm eggs for her.

"Eat," he said.

She smiled gratefully, eating her eggs obediently. Her thoughts stubbornly circled around last evening. She had never thought to see this side of her most beloved sister. Perhaps some matters of one's life should stay private, and not even the closest ones should look into them?

Elizabeth was rather surprised when after breakfast Darcy announced that they would take a walk in the park before the ladies' departure to Longbourn. It was said in such a tone that no one doubted that he wished for privacy, and did not invite anyone else on to join them.

She was surprised with the abruptness of his tone and manner, but did not protest when he helped her into her coat, accepting his arm as he led them outside. As soon as they were on the lane which curved in a large irregular circle around the house, he released her arm, and facing her, his tone serious, asked, "Have I upset you with my behaviour?"

Surprised with his question, she did not answer instantly.

"Was I too forward last night?" he questioned, his expression strained.

"No, no, no," she answered, shaking her head. "It was a lovely evening," she assured.

His face and body relaxed visibly. With a smile, she stepped closer to him, placing her cheek on his chest. His arms went around her and he kissed the top of her head. It was a sound idea that she had forgone on putting the bonnet on.

"When you were so quiet at breakfast, barely acknowledging me, I began to think that I offended you last night."

"Far from that," she said, tilting her head to look at him. "I felt like the happiest woman in all England."

He let out a relieved sigh. "This betrothal business is still very new to me. I do not wish to make you dislike me again."

She stared at him, speechless for a moment. She had not expected such words from him. "It is not possible, Fitzwilliam. I cannot promise not to ever become cross about something, angry or disappointed. But I love you; I cannot think of anything that you could do to undo it. As you are the best of men, my love for you will only grow."

Bending his head down, he touched her lips gently with his. Elizabeth wished for a longer kiss, but as they were in open view, she knew that it would not happen.

"You were sad at breakfast, though. Is something worrying you? If you share it with me, perhaps I can help you," he said, resuming their walk.

"Can you not guess? I was thinking about Jane and Mr. Bingley."

"Why about them?"

She stopped moving, staring at him in astonishment. "How can you ask, after what we witnessed last night?"

Darcy frowned, looking down at her with concern. "You are not afraid that he hurt her, are you? I can assure you that as far as I know, Bingley would never harm a lady. You also should remember that your sister was a willing participant last night, from what I noticed. She was not coerced by him in any way."

"It never crossed my mind that she was!" she exclaimed.

"I do not understand, then."

"I was shocked with what I saw. Jane is always so composed, so very proper. It was very much out of character."

"Elizabeth, your sister is a young and healthy woman who is engaged and in love with a handsome young man. I believe that what we witnessed was perfectly normal, nothing out of the ordinary, and nothing that you should worry yourself over."

"Should I talk to her about it?"

"I would advise you do not."

"Why?"

"It is a private matter between Bingley and your sister. You should not question her about it unless she begins to talk about it first, which I sincerely doubt."

"Jane and I have always shared everything."

"Still, I would caution you against speaking to her about it. Let me remind you that what she and Bingley do behind closed doors is entirely their business."

"You do not understand," Elizabeth insisted. "She is my most beloved sister."

"I do understand. I have a close friendship with Bingley, and an even closer one with Colonel Fitzwilliam. However, I do firmly believe that there are matters which are too intimate to mention. Even though I confessed to Colonel Fitzwilliam the story of your rejection of my first proposal, I would never think it appropriate or necessary to share the intimate details of our relationship with him. I know that he does not expect me to, and he would never ask about it."

Elizabeth nodded at his reasoning, but she was not convinced. They walked in silence for some time when Darcy stopped abruptly, asking, "You are not jealous, are you?"

"No!" she cried out. "Of course not! I was only concerned and surprised." She did not know why, but she found it very difficult at the moment to look into his eyes. She felt him putting his finger under her chin, forcing her to look at him.

He stared into her eyes for the longest time, not allowing her to break the contact. "I love you passionately, Elizabeth Bennet."

She rolled her eyes at him. "I do know of that."

"I do not think that you truly do. Have you forgotten what happened in Netherfield's library at the very beginning of our engagement?"

"I do remember, but since then you have barely touched me," she complained.

"You must understand why I keep my distance."

"I am not certain I do."

He sighed. "Elizabeth, I simply do not wish for us to lose control. We are not yet married."

"Is that the only reason?"

"Darling, I wanted you in my bed before I realized that I loved you, and well before I even began to consider marrying you."

She tilted her head to the side. "It is difficult to believe."

"Believe me, then. You must have noticed my constant staring, my hostility towards you."

"You did not like me back then."

"I did not like Caroline Bingley. I could not care less whether she was in the same room with me or not. But when you were near, I had to clench my hands into fists to stop myself from touching you. My regard for you had always been passionate, almost from the first moments of our acquaintance. May I remind you how I asked you to consider elopement on the third day in our engagement?"

"It was a jest on your part."

He shook his head. "It was not, I was perfectly serious. I was ready to put a blemish on my family name with the stigma of Gretna Green only so I could have you as my wife sooner."

"Apart from that morning in the library, we never touch the way Jane and Mr. Bingley did last night," she complained.

"Because once we start, I do not think that either you or I would be able to stop. It is not my wish for everyone in

Derbyshire to gossip that the new heir to Pemberley was born two months earlier than he should have."

"I am not naive. I was raised in the country, if I may remind you. Moreover, I have read some books from Papa's library which I probably should not have. I do know very well that a child will not come from kissing and touching."

"No, but it may surely come from this," he grunted, pulling her to him a bit roughly. One of his hands rested firmly around her waist, the other arm lowered down considerably, pressing there. He lifted her up at the same time so that the tips of her feet were dangling in the air a few inches above the ground. Her eyes widened dramatically as she felt the change in his body prominently pressing into her lower stomach. "I beg you not to torture me with such discussions, as I will be forced to put on fresh trousers, which I am always very embarrassed to do."

He put her abruptly down and marched away from her, the ends of his great coat blowing behind him. After a long moment of standing speechless on the lane, she moved her legs, running after him. "Fitzwilliam!" she cried as she caught up to him, tugging at his arm.

He stopped, glaring at her.

"I wish for you to touch me, hold me and kiss me," she said. "I crave it. I trust you that you can be careful enough to avoid unwanted—for now, at least—consequences."

He considered for a moment before he gave her his answer. "Once we are in London, I will try to arrange some time alone for us. However, I do not promise anything to you."

Elizabeth rose on her toes, wrapping her arms around his neck. "Thank you," she whispered.

"Let us go," he spoke gruffly, offering his arm to her. "They are surely waiting for us."

CHAPTER SEVEN

"I must say, Lizzy, that I was not overly surprised when the news of your engagement reached us," Mrs. Gardiner said with a kind smile on her face.

Mrs. Bennet, Elizabeth, and Jane, as well as all the Gardiner children, were seated at the large table enjoying a late breakfast. Mr. Gardiner had left home hours ago, having many meetings planned since the early morning.

"I was most surprised!" Mrs. Bennet exclaimed, having swallowed the last piece of sweet croissant. "I always thought that Mr. Darcy did not like our Lizzy."

"I met Mr. Darcy when we were touring Pemberley," Mrs. Gardiner reminded. "He was such a gracious host to us even though we were perfect strangers to him. It was not even an hour into our stay there when I understood that it was because of Lizzy we had received such a warm welcome from him."

Mrs. Bennet looked at her second daughter with large, round eyes. "Lizzy, you never told me that you visited Pemberley."

"There was no occasion for that, Mama," Elizabeth said. "It was at Lambton, only five miles from Pemberley, when we received the news of Lydia's elopement. It was because of that less-than-pleasant experience that we had to interrupt our stay."

"Less than pleasant? Why are you saying that, Lizzy? In my view it was terribly romantic. I swear that every mother in Hertfordshire is envious of me, considering the excellent matches that my daughters have made so far. Mr. Wickham may not be as rich as Mr. Bingley or Darcy, but I am certain that he will do a career in the army, especially with our dear Lydia at his side. Elopements are in fashion today, and I am certain that many mothers of young ladies in the neighbourhood wish for their daughters to be abducted by some handsome officer the same as our dear Lydia was."

Elizabeth stared at her mother, not fully believing what she had just heard. Since her and Jane's engagement, Mrs. Bennet's demeanour was vastly improved. She was always cheerful and smiling. However, when it came to overall silliness and stupidity, she had not been permanently cured of those.

Elizabeth was about to respond sharply to the nonsense that came from her mother's mouth when she felt Jane reaching for her hand and giving it a light squeeze. Taking a calming breath, she counted to ten, fighting the urge to bash her mother. She knew that it would give no result. Mrs. Bennet was incorrigible. No matter what Elizabeth said, she would always think of Lydia as the best of her daughters, even though the girl had nearly ruined their entire family with her selfishness and recklessness. If not for Darcy, neither of the Bennet sisters would now have a chance for a good marriage, or any marriage at all. Whereas Lydia would be living in disgrace, not being admitted in polite society.

"Tell me, Sister, what are your ideas for Jane and Elizabeth's wedding gowns?" Mrs. Gardiner asked, clearly wishing to change the topic of the conversation, bringing it to safer shores. "I am very curious."

Mrs. Bennet went off immediately about what designs she was considering. Soon they were looking through many fashion magazines which Mrs. Gardiner had in her collection.

Elizabeth breathed in relief that the attention was taken away from her. She looked at Jane gratefully. Her sister read her well and always knew when she was about to lose her patience with their mother. She would miss Jane very much once she moved north after the wedding.

She was glad that she listened to Darcy and did not try to discuss with Jane what she had witnessed that night at Netherfield. After longer consideration, she had to admit that Darcy was perfectly right in pointing out that it was too intimate a matter to discuss without any encouragement from Jane. As her sister never brought the subject up, it was left to Elizabeth to stay silent about it.

It was the second day of their stay in London. She had not seen Darcy since the day before yesterday and she was already longing for his company. He was in London with Georgiana and Mr. Bingley, and they were to dine at Darcy's townhouse tomorrow evening.

As soon as they had arrived yesterday evening, Mrs. Bennet had announced that she had no intention to waste any of the precious time during their stay in London. They were to start visiting shops today. Mrs. Gardiner would not be able to join them. Elizabeth understood that her aunt, being almost seven months pregnant with her fourth child, could hardly venture for long and tiresome trips, but nevertheless she would have preferred for her to join them. Her presence would make the day much more bearable. Contrary to her sisters, shopping for gowns, hats, shoes and gloves was her least favourite pastime. She would much prefer to visit some of the town's best bookshops.

Nevertheless, she had to admit that her mother had an excellent taste in clothes. Mrs. Bennet had the ability to pick up materials and designs which looked more expensive than they truly were.

Elizabeth expected the day to be long, tiresome and tedious, but it proved to be much worse. At first she was surprised when Mrs. Bennet ordered to drive them to Bond Street, where most of the shops were above their financial means. She had expected that they would go to the seamstress not far from Cheapside which Mrs. Gardiner frequented.

Her astonishment only grew when her mother entered the

expensive-looking shop with tall windows right in the middle of Bond Street. Mrs. Bennet walked up to an elegant but severely dressed lady, who turned out to be the owner of the establishment, talking to her quietly. It was rather strange, as her mother rarely used shushed tones when addressing anyone.

Soon, Elizabeth, Jane, and Mrs. Bennet were seated on the sofa, tea and refreshments served to them while they looked at the many materials and designs. Elizabeth grew alarmed when she saw the quality of the materials which her mother had been selecting. She knew that their father had no money to pay for all these. What was her mother thinking? "Mama, are you certain that Papa can afford it?" she whispered in her mother's ear.

Mrs. Bennet kept smiling at the owner, who was discussing what kind of fur should be used for Elizabeth's winter coat. She would need one for the much colder weather in the north. "Surely you do not think that your father is paying for all this?" Mrs. Bennet whispered back, before asking loudly how long it would take to finish the coat and whether there was the possibility of sending it directly to Derbyshire.

Elizabeth sat numbly for a moment longer, not saying a single word. The emotions which she felt were many, and none of them were pleasant. Embarrassment and humiliation were the strongest. Had her mother talked Darcy into it? Had she accosted him to pay for all those clothes? She would have thought her mother to have more tact. They were not beggars, and she would be perfectly happy with less expensive gowns made by Mrs. Gardiner's seamstress.

Barely paying attention to what was spoken around her, she was led away into another room and asked to undress. While her measurements were taken, she wondered why Jane did not join her in here. Only then it struck her that Jane was not picking any materials for herself today, she only advised what should suit Elizabeth. Poor Jane! She was sitting there, looking pleased and content, even though none of those lovely things would be for her.

Elizabeth could not wait for them to leave the shop. As soon as they were inside the carriage, she turned to Mrs. Bennet. "Mama, did you talk Mr. Darcy into this?"

"What are you speaking of?"

"Did you talk him into paying for my new dresses?"

"I did not. He approached me about it himself. He gave me the address of the shop that we have just been to, saying that his sister frequented it and it was all settled to put your expenses on his account."

"Why did you not refuse him?"

Her mother stared at her with amazement. "Refuse such a kind offer? Why would I do such a thing?"

"Do you not posses any pride, Mother?"

"Lizzy!" Jane exclaimed softly. "I am certain that Mama only wished for the best."

"Listen to your sister for once, Elizabeth," Mrs. Bennet said. "By accepting Mr. Darcy's generosity we can afford better gowns for Jane."

"I would much prefer to have lesser dresses but from the same seamstress as my sister," Elizabeth argued.

"You will be mistress of a grand estate and you have to look like one. What would the servants think if you arrived there in the second-best dresses in your trunk?"

"I do not care! You humiliated me!"

"What are you speaking of?" Mrs. Bennet enquired, looking truly concerned. "Truly, Elizabeth, sometimes I am worried that you are becoming mentally deranged."

"Lizzy, Lizzy, look at me," Jane said, forcefully reaching for both of Elizabeth's hands. "We will talk about it later tonight. You must calm down. Both Mr. Darcy and Mama had only your best interest at heart."

Elizabeth nodded slowly. She glanced over at her mother, who looked both terrified and greatly worried.

"I think that it is best we return home now," Jane proposed. "We shall start again early in the morning tomorrow."

"Very well, Jane," Mrs. Bennet agreed, stealing wary glances at her second daughter, who was sitting quietly, staring down at her hands.

Once they returned to Cheapside, Mrs. Gardiner was

awaiting them impatiently, wishing to hear all the news about the shopping they had accomplished today.

Elizabeth excused herself as soon as she could, citing a headache. Mrs. Gardiner gave her a concerned but understanding look. She knew that shopping was not Elizabeth's favourite activity.

***

Elizabeth was resting calmly on the bed even though her insides were in turmoil. It felt very wrong to her that Darcy was paying for her clothes before the wedding. She could not think about it otherwise or rationalize his deed in her mind in any way. She was hardly surprised with her mother's ready acceptance of Darcy's offer. However, she could not believe that Darcy had come with such an idea on his own, presenting it to Mrs. Bennet behind Elizabeth's back without her knowledge. Did he not understand that she already felt indebted to him for dealing with Wickham and all the money he had spent to force him into marrying Lydia?

She did not open her eyes when she heard a knock at the door, followed by someone entering the room. She guessed that it was Jane, but she did not wish to talk even to her sister at the present moment.

"Lizzy, my dear, how are you feeling?"

Elizabeth opened her eyes to see Mrs. Bennet standing next to the bed. She could not remember the last time when her mother had come to see her when she had been upset.

Then Mrs. Bennet leaned down, whispering, "Mr. Darcy and Mr. Bingley have just arrived. Mr. Darcy is here. When he heard that you were unwell he insisted on seeing you. Have mercy on us all and be polite to him."

Elizabeth sat up, watching as her mother walked to the door, opening it wide to let Darcy in.

"Thank you, Mrs. Bennet," Darcy responded as the woman left them alone, closing the door after herself.

Elizabeth put her legs on the floor, sitting up.

Darcy made his way to her with haste. "How are you feeling?" he enquired, cupping her cheek. "They told me that you had a headache."

"Shopping is not a favourite pastime of mine," she explained quietly, enjoying his touch on her skin.

He stared into her face for a moment longer before leading them to the small sofa only large enough to accommodate two people. He sat down first, pulling her onto his lap. "Has something upset you?" he enquired. "Your mother?"

Elizabeth pulled back to look into his eyes. "Mama said that you offered to pay for my dresses."

"I did."

"Why did you do it?"

"I do not understand."

"Why did you make such an offer to her? You must have

guessed that she would agree."

"Why should I not? I assumed that it would be convenient for you to make your purchases at the same shop where Georgiana does hers. If you do not like this seamstress, you can look for someone different."

"You have already spent a fortune to pay off Wickham, to rescue Lydia's reputation. And now this? Can you imagine how humiliated I felt today when I realized that all the bills would be sent directly to you?" She got off his lap, walking to the window.

"Be reasonable, Elizabeth. In two months we shall be married."

"We are not married yet."

He stood as well, and began pacing the room. "I do not see what is upsetting you so much."

"How can you not see it? Imagine Georgiana or even our own daughter in such a situation in the years to come. Would you allow their betrotheds to pay for their expenses before the wedding?"

"Of course not. However, our situation is entirely different. Our daughter or Georgiana will never lack in any way, especially when it comes to purchasing a few gowns."

"I do not see it to be different. My father has money to pay for my expenses. I would be much happier with the dresses bought at the shop where my aunt does hers."

"In Cheapside?"

The way he said 'Cheapside' stung. Elizabeth grimaced inwardly. It was the same tone which Caroline Bingley had used once when referring to her aunt and uncle's place of residence.

"Yes, in Cheapside," she responded. "Mrs. Gardiner is a very elegant woman, you cannot deny that."

"Elizabeth, I can hardly believe that we are even discussing it," he said, coming to stand in front of her. "Let me explain. You are about to enter a different social sphere and you must look the part of my wife. Your father cannot afford to pay for the right kind of clothes for you, especially with Jane's expenses coming at the same time. By offering to take care of your account now, I was thinking ahead. Once we are at Pemberley, I wish to concentrate solely on my wife, on spending time with her in my ancestral home. I do not wish to worry that I need to take her to town when she needs new gowns because the ones that she has are more suited for my housekeeper than the mistress of Pemberley. I simply want to have you all to myself for those first months. I want for us to stay home and enjoy our privacy."

Elizabeth looked down at her hands. Darcy was rich, but she had never felt as inferior to him as now, not even when she had visited Pemberley for the first time, seeing its grandeur. Had he truly seen her like that from the beginning of their acquaintance? As the girl dressed too poorly to stand by his side?

His arms went around her. "Please, Elizabeth, no more of this," he spoke gently, touching her cheek. "We cannot allow such a silly matter to ruin our happiness. I do appreciate your independence and pride, but it is not needed here. We both know that you are not marrying me because of my fortune. You would not have refused me so decidedly the first time if it were the case. Please," he whispered, touching her lips with his. When she did not respond, he pulled back. "I came here today because I could not live another hour without seeing you, and this is the welcome I am receiving?"

She smiled at him then, but it was unconvincing even to her.

Darcy was not deterred with her lack of enthusiasm. He kissed her again, more deeply this time.

A knock at the door made them stop their amorous activities.

Jane's clear, high voice was heard. "Lizzy, Aunt is inviting Mr. Darcy and you to join us for tea in the drawing room."

"Yes, Jane. We shall come downstairs in a moment."

Darcy groaned, hiding his face in the curve of her neck.

"Less than two months, less than two months," she heard him murmuring.

"Two months?" she asked.

"Our wedding," he explained, straightening up his tall frame.

"I am beginning to think that the engagement is the least pleasant part out of the entire courtship."

"You are not enjoying it?" she asked, walking to the mirror on the wall to repin some curls which had escaped the bun. Darcy joined her, standing behind her, watching the back of her neck.

"It is frustrating. You are mine, but still I cannot spend as much time with you as I would wish to."

Elizabeth turned to face him. "As you said, it will be in less than two months."

He leaned down to kiss her forehead. "Let us hurry, or they will start looking for us again."

Elizabeth accepted his arm, allowing him to lead them downstairs. She was still not pleased about his unneeded—in her opinion—generosity. However, although she still did not like what he had done, she decided to reconsider it before returning to this topic again.

She would talk with Jane tonight. Her sister was always capable of offering sound advice on such matters.

***

"Why should you feel humiliated, Lizzy?" Jane asked her later that night.

The sisters sat on the bed in their nightclothes, the single candle illuminating the room. They had to share the room, as the Gardiners did not have enough guest chambers to put them separately.

"He should not have said to Mama that he would pay for the dresses, knowing well that she would have never refused such an offer."

"I am certain that it was not Mr. Darcy's intention to offend you in any way."

"But he did," Elizabeth argued. "He made me feel inferior when he said that my gowns were more suitable for his housekeeper than a mistress of Pemberley."

"It was inconsiderate of him to say that, but Lizzy, he is not perfect, no one is. I do think that his intentions were good."

"I should forget about it, then?" Elizabeth asked.

"You should make him aware if there is something which you dislike in his behaviour. However, I do not think that it is a good idea to return to it over and over again like Mama does when Papa acts in a way which she dislikes."

Elizabeth nodded her head. She was determined to avoid her mother's mistakes in her own marriage.

"I do believe that in time Mr. Darcy will become more sensitive to your needs and feelings. Do not be too harsh on him. I do not believe that he would ever offend you purposely."

Elizabeth sighed. "You are right, Jane, as always. You are always taking into consideration every perspective first before making a judgement. I wish to be more like you, but I allow my feelings and emotions to rule me so very often."

"One cannot change one's nature. Mr. Darcy likes you the way you are. You should follow his example in that respect."

CHAPTER EIGHT

The following day Elizabeth began with the new resolution to enjoy it as much as possible even though there was more shopping planned. They spent the entire morning and most of the afternoon in the company of the seamstress Mrs. Gardiner favoured, discussing the dresses for Jane. Elizabeth felt much happier and more comfortable when her elder sister was in the centre of attention instead of her. Jane looked beautiful in most colours and designs, thus it was difficult to limit her selections to only a few to suit her the best.

They returned home well after three in the afternoon, which left them a little time to rest and prepare themselves for dinner at Darcy's townhouse. It had been agreed yesterday that Darcy would send his carriage for Elizabeth, Jane, and Mrs. Bennet.

Jane and Elizabeth were dressing themselves in their bedroom when their mother entered, announcing that she was unable to accompany them. She claimed a severe headache prevented her from joining her daughters. Elizabeth had no other choice but to believe that her mother was truly unwell, as she could not imagine that Mrs. Bennet would voluntarily forego attending dinner in Mayfair.

It was promptly decided that Jane and Elizabeth should not go alone, thus Mr. Gardiner was asked to escort them. However, he excused himself from the task, quoting tiredness. Elizabeth and Jane had decided to go alone when Mrs. Gardiner volunteered to join them. She was eager to escape the house after being closed up for the last several months. While it was not customary for a woman so far in her condition to attend parties, they were invited to a private house, about to spend the evening within a small circle of close friends soon to become family, thus it did not seem inappropriate.

Elizabeth and Jane welcomed Mrs. Gardiner warmly into their company with both enthusiasm and a degree of quiet relief. Their mother, although always devoted to accompanying her daughters to social meetings, was often a source of acute embarrassment for the sisters. With Mrs Gardiner in attendance they had no such fears.

They were to arrive at Darcy's townhouse at six, but as Mrs. Gardiner needed more time to prepare herself, it was nearly half past when the carriage stopped in front of a tall, white town house.

Elizabeth had never seen it before, and even though it was not the largest out of the ones lining the street, she could hardly call it 'modest,' as Darcy persistently referred to it

. "There you are!" Mr. Bingley exclaimed, hurrying out of the front entrance with Darcy close behind him. "We were worried that something unfortunate had happened."

"Mama felt unwell and could not attend," Jane explained as she accepted Bingley's hand, stepping out of the carriage. "Mrs. Gardiner agreed to join us for the evening."

"Excellent! Excellent!" Mr. Bingley exclaimed, even though soon he realized that his enthusiasm was perhaps not in place. "I do hope that Mrs. Bennet will soon feel better," he added with feeling, trying to cover his earlier blunder.

"She is exhausted and needed rest more than anything," Elizabeth assured.

With great care Mr. Darcy helped Mrs. Gardiner down, offering his arm to her. "It is a great pleasure to welcome you in my home," he spoke with sincerity.

Mrs. Gardiner thanked him with a smile and together they entered the house.

Their outer clothing was promptly taken away and they were led upstairs to the reception room situated on the first floor.

Elizabeth entered the tall and long room furnished with sofas, settees, and chairs as well as smaller and bigger tables. She found it perfect for entertaining guests.

Georgiana sprang to her feet to greet them, and it was only after they had settled down on the sofas in the middle of the room when Elizabeth noticed another woman sitting opposite them.

"Good evening, Eliza," Caroline Bingley said. "I did not expect to see you here."

Elizabeth nodded her head at the tall redhead in acknowledgment of her company but said nothing in return. She did not know why Miss Bingley was here, but she had no intention of having a conversation with her. All too well she remembered her role in separating Mr. Bingley from Jane.

Jane, being her good and kind self, began speaking to Caroline. However, Elizabeth noticed that her sister was quite reserved and cautious in her manner and words. Caroline on her part was polite towards her future sister but hardly enthusiastic.

Elizabeth concentrated her attention on Georgiana and Mrs. Gardiner, but with the corner of her eye she caught a glimpse of Miss Bingley's attire. She was dressed in an elaborate bright green dress with orange ribbons and an orange turban with green feathers. It hurt one's eyes to look at this ensemble for longer than a short moment.

Elizabeth found it very rude that Caroline entirely ignored Mrs. Gardiner. She should have at the very least acknowledged an older married woman with a polite greeting.

Georgiana and Mrs. Gardiner were engaged in an animated conversation. Elizabeth, assured that her aunt was in good company, made her way to Darcy, who stood by the fireplace, talking with his friend. As soon as Mr. Bingley saw her approaching, he excused himself to give them some privacy. He took a seat next to Jane, listening to her conversation with his sister.

"Are you well, my love?" Darcy asked, following her gaze as she stared at Jane and Caroline.

"Why is she here?"

"Bingley told me that she returned from Scarborough earlier today, unannounced. It seems that their relatives could not bear her for much longer, and she longed for London. I understand that she is here on the condition she be kind to Jane. Charles is in charge of her inheritance and monthly allowance, after all, and I daresay that he was forced to remind her of that."

Elizabeth nodded in understanding while her eyes were on Jane.

"Do not be concerned, Caroline has too much to lose to misbehave now."

At last Elizabeth tore her attention away from the other end of the room, looking back at Darcy. "It was a rather unwelcome surprise to meet her here."

"I could not forbid her from coming," he explained. "I am afraid that we will have to welcome her at Pemberley occasionally."

"Not too often, I hope."

Darcy reached his hand to touch her shoulder, stroking it in a soothing motion. "Do not allow her person to bother you."

"I cannot forget how she betrayed Jane's trust. She befriended her to amuse herself only to abandon her when Jane was no longer needed. I can only hope that Jane will be more careful this time."

"Jane needs to be civil to Caroline, as they will be sisters. However, I doubt that she will allow herself to be fooled by her one more time."

"I do hope so."

"Let us change the subject," Darcy proposed. "Can I offer you anything to drink before dinner?"

"A glass of wine, perhaps?"

"A half glass," he agreed, stepping to the small table which hosted various drinks and glasses. "You should not drink too much, especially not on an empty stomach. We both know how it will end."

Elizabeth rolled her eyes at him. "We both know that the wine you gave me that night was quite strong."

"That was my mistake," he agreed, handing her the glass half filled with red liquid. "This one is milder."

Elizabeth took a sip. "It is sweet as well, I like it."

"It is Georgiana's favourite."

Elizabeth enjoyed her drink, sipping slowly as Darcy stood close to her, his hand placed on the small of her back, his thumb drawing small circles, making her warm inside and a little drowsy. She could feel someone's gaze burning into her back, and as she glanced back she saw Caroline Bingley staring daggers in her direction.

"Tired?" he asked, pulling her closer into his embrace, draping his arm behind her back.

"We picked quite a few dresses for Jane today, but it consumed almost the entire morning and most of the afternoon."

"Successful day, then?"

"Yes, but there are many purchases yet to be done in the following days. I am not surprised that Mama developed a headache."

"Perhaps you should rest for a day or two."

"Oh, no, Mama will not hear of it. She is like a general planning the campaign before the battle. Nothing will deter her from her task until the wedding day arrives."

Loud cries coming from the other side interrupted them. "Charles, Charles, is that the truth?" Caroline demanded. "Tell me this instant!"

Mr. Bingley mumbled something, but Elizabeth only saw his mouth move and was not able to understand much. Caroline stood up with such force that the chair on which she was seated fell backwards. Elizabeth watched as she marched towards them, her face red, her expression furious.

"You!" she exclaimed, pointing at Elizabeth. "Your fault!"

Elizabeth's eyes widened as she looked up at Darcy, who stood calmly by her side.

"It has been your doing! Everything!" Caroline accused, her chest heaving. "Crass, coarse and vulgar, with no consequence to the world! How dare you! You are no one. He will hate you!" She pointed to Darcy this time. "He will hate you," she repeated. "His family will never accept you! You will ruin him!"

Elizabeth had no opportunity to react to such an outburst of violence and fury because Darcy stepped decidedly in front of her, protecting her from Caroline's assault.

"Madam, I must ask you to leave my home," he spoke in a deep, cold voice.

"You must come to your senses, Darcy!" Caroline insisted. "She made a fool of you! Can you not see it?"

Darcy took a step forward. "Leave now or I will have the butler throw you out on the street," he threatened.

"Caroline, that is quite enough!"

Elizabeth looked in amazement at Mr. Bingley, who suddenly appeared by their side. She had never heard him speaking in such a firm voice. His sister, however, decided to ignore him and surged forward, attempting with her outstretched hands to reach Elizabeth past Darcy's broad shoulder.

Caroline let out a long screech as her brother wrapped his arms around her waist, dragging her away from Darcy and Elizabeth.

Silence fell in the room, but the sounds of Caroline's shrieks were still heard throughout the house.

"Excuse me," Darcy said, walking stiffly out of the room.

Elizabeth slowly returned to her previous place, sitting by her aunt.

It was Jane who spoke first. "Caroline was not aware of your engagement, Lizzy."

"How could she not?" Elizabeth enquired.

"She has been in the north with her aunt for the last two months. Mr. Bingley informed her of our engagement, but he neglected to tell her of yours with Mr. Darcy."

"He should have told her," Mrs. Gardiner said grimly. "We might have been spared this pitiful and embarrassing scene."

Georgiana stood up and walked to the window, pushing away the curtain to look down at the street. "Mr. Bingley is putting Miss Bingley into the carriage. My brother is with them."

Mrs. Gardiner touched Elizabeth's arm. "How are you feeling, Lizzy?"

Elizabeth smiled bravely. "I certainly had not expected such an outcome this evening."

"That woman is out of her mind," Mrs. Gardiner stated.

"It was quite a surprise for her, I believe," Jane spoke, looking apologetically at her sister, moving to sit on her other side. "Aunt is right. Charles should have informed her about your engagement before bringing her here."

"Perhaps he should have, but he had no responsibility to do that," Mrs. Gardiner said. "And she should not have behaved in such a way upon hearing the news. Elizabeth's engagement is not a concern of hers."

Georgiana returned to her seat, looking over the three women seated closely together on one sofa. "Should I play some music?" she asked quietly, interrupting the silence.

Mrs. Gardiner kindly smiled at her. "Yes, dear, that would be lovely."

Within a minute the music began. Georgiana's long fingers were flying over the white and black keys, but Elizabeth could barely concentrate her attention on the beautiful composition. She had known that Caroline Bingley disliked her. However, she would have never expected such an outburst on her part. She felt for Jane. She could not imagine how her sister should behave in this situation. After all, Caroline was her future sister, and that could not be changed. She would not disappear from their lives.

Georgiana finished playing, and shortly after, dinner was announced. They decided to eat, not waiting for Darcy, as it was impossible to guess how soon he would return. The conversation at the table concerned shopping and the plans for the rest of their stay in London. None of the ladies mentioned Caroline and what happened before.

It was quite late in the evening when Mrs. Gardiner decided that it was high time for them to go back to Cheapside. As the ladies were putting on their coats and bonnets in the foyer, dutifully accompanied by Georgiana, Darcy entered the house.

"You are leaving already?" he spoke.

"It is nearly ten in the evening, Mr. Darcy," Mrs. Gardiner pointed out gently.

Darcy stepped towards the older woman, although his eyes were focused on Elizabeth. "Allow me to apologize for what transpired earlier this evening. Had I known, had I predicted, I would have never allowed Miss Bingley to join us tonight, or any other occasion for that matter."

"The fault is not yours, Mr. Darcy," Mrs. Gardiner assured him with smile. "None of us could have guessed that we might witness such an unpleasant event. Pray tell me, how is that poor woman feeling?"

"Poor woman?" Elizabeth snorted, challenging her aunt with a fierce stare of her dark green eyes.

"Anyone who acts in such a way in public cannot be entirely sane, Lizzy," Mrs. Gardiner justified.

"Definitely not quite right in her mind."

"I believe that you are correct, Mrs. Gardiner," Darcy agreed with her. "Miss Bingley was in hysterics during the short carriage ride, and she did not calm herself after arriving at their residence. Bingley was forced to ask me to bring the physician."

"Is she any better?" Jane asked.

"I do not know. I left soon after I brought the physician for her. I believe that Miss Bingley suffered from a mental breakdown of sorts. Let us hope that the physician will manage to help her."

"Yes, let us hope that Miss Bingley will feel better soon," Mrs. Gardiner said before glancing at her nieces. "Ladies, it is high time for us to leave. Mr. Gardiner must be worried why we have not returned yet."

The whole company walked out to the awaiting carriage. Darcy first handed Mrs. Gardiner, then Jane and his betrothed. He held Elizabeth's hand longer, saying quietly, "Forgive me, dearest."

"It is not your fault, Fitzwilliam."

"I should have reacted sooner, asked her to leave before she had opportunity to speak to you."

"Will I see you tomorrow?"

He nodded. "I will come around four."

"We will be home."

Darcy shut the door and Elizabeth watched him standing on the pavement, watching their carriage driving away.

On the way to Cheapside, the ladies decided that there was no point in informing Mrs. Bennet about exactly what had happened that evening. It was enough to say that Miss Bingley had simply felt unwell and was forced to return home earlier than the rest of the company.

CHAPTER NINE

The next day, both Elizabeth and Jane woke up quite late. Their shopping plans had to be delayed until midday. At breakfast, Mrs. Bennet was very curious about their visit to the Darcy townhouse, asking detailed questions about the size of the rooms, the number of servants and the food which was served.

"Miss Bingley was there, then?" Mrs. Bennet asked, eyeing her eldest daughter.

Jane nodded. "Yes, she was, Mama."

"Was she pleasant to you?"

The sisters exchanged a quick look before Jane answered, "Quite pleasant. However, she became unwell shortly before dinner was served, and Mr. Bingley had to escort her home."

"Did he return later on? From what I understand, his residence is quite close to Darcy's."

"He did not return, Mama."

Mrs. Bennet shook her head in displeasure. "I do not like it, Jane. If he left before dinner, you spent no time with him at all. I hope that Caroline Bingley is not trying to separate her brother from you again. I remember all too well how she snubbed you last winter. She befriended you only to abandon you later, taking Mr. Bingley away with her."

"I do not believe that is the case now, Mama."

"Mr. Bingley should put his foot down with her. He controls her expenses, after all. It would be enough to cut her monthly allowance to remind her of her place. I will have to talk to him about it personally."

"I beg you not to do it," Jane pleaded. "I am certain that Charles knows what he is doing when it comes to his sister."

Mrs. Bennet reached her hand to touch her eldest daughter's smooth, creamy cheek. "You are too good, Jane, much too good and kind. You will be Mrs. Charles Bingley in a short time, and Caroline must understand that you will be in charge from now on, and not her. As for Caroline's expenses, I firmly believe that Mr. Bingley gives her too much pocket money. At her age she should start looking for a husband, not living off her brother, who will soon have his own family with its own needs."

"I beg you, Mama, not to discuss this with Mr. Bingley," Jane repeated.

"Do not fret, Jane. I can be a diplomat when there is such a need. I will find just the right moment to express my worries to Mr. Bingley. However, I cannot allow some spinster like Caroline Bingley to influence the relationship with your husband. I will not allow my girls to be harmed in any way."

With those words Mrs. Bennet looked around the table with

triumph in her big blue eyes. The Gardiners chose to stay silent, abstaining from offering their opinion. Mr. Gardiner was reading his morning newspaper, frowning over some article, while his wife was quietly guiding their youngest boy on how to handle the fork without spilling the eggs all over his clothes. The older children were busy with their food, taught from the earliest age that they should be seen but not heard at the table during the meal.

Elizabeth considered reasoning with her mother that it was not her place to advise Mr. Bingley on how he should treat his sister, but in the end she decided that her intervention would bring more harm than good. Moreover, she agreed wholeheartedly with Mrs. Bennet that Caroline Bingley should not be trusted.

Jane stared at her plate, red faced, sad and embarrassed. Elizabeth did not envy her. While Elizabeth was gaining a new sister in Georgiana, a kind and intelligent young lady who would be an excellent companion and a friend, Jane was faced with entering the family where Caroline would be every day a nuisance. Mrs. Bennet was right that it would be much easier for Jane if Caroline got engaged and married. There was little chance, though, that it would happen anytime soon. Caroline's personality and behaviour was scaring reasonable men away from her. Moreover, Miss Bingley wished to become Mrs. Darcy of Pemberley, and Elizabeth doubted that would change in the near future.

***

Elizabeth, Jane and Mrs. Bennet returned from their shopping trip that day a mere quarter of an hour before Darcy and Bingley arrived to visit the ladies. When the gentlemen arrived, Mrs. Gardiner was busy with the children; Mr. Gardiner was away, inspecting the warehouses; and Mrs. Bennet decided that she was too tired to stay with the guests.

Elizabeth was grateful to her mother that she had left them alone, and she knew that Jane shared her feelings. Mrs. Bennet always made sure that her eldest daughters could spend as much private time with their future husbands as it was possible, often bending the rules of propriety.

"How is Caroline feeling?" Jane asked as soon as they were left alone.

"Not too well, I am afraid," Mr. Bingley said. "There is some improvement from yesterday. She is not weeping anymore. She stares at some point in front of her, not answering any questions, refusing to eat."

"What is the physician's opinion?" Elizabeth asked.

"Nervous breakdown. We explained the situation to him, and he interpreted it in such a way; for the last couple of years Caroline put all her efforts, thoughts and attention into becoming Mrs. Darcy. In her mind she had already seen herself as such. When she suddenly learned that another woman replaced her, she lost control over herself."

"She is truly ill," Jane spoke with concern.

"I am very worried," Mr. Bingley said, his expression grave. "No one in our family has ever suffered from mental illness. I fear that her state will only deteriorate."

"A change of scenery might help," Elizabeth suggested.

"Indeed it might. The physician said exactly the same. Unfortunately, Caroline cannot go alone. Mrs. Hurst is currently with child, and as they have been waiting for so long to become parents, my brother refused to allow her to exert herself now. Also, I am afraid that our relatives in Scarborough will be most reluctant to invite her again, especially in her current state. She was less than pleasant during her last stay there. No one is missing her."

"You have to go with your sister," Jane stated calmly.

Bingley moved to sit next to her, taking her hand in both of his. "Dearest Jane, I simply have to go with her. I cannot leave her now. I thought that Ramsgate or some other quiet seaside village should be suitable to calm her nerves."

"It is only natural that you have to go," Jane agreed with him. "I would have done exactly the same for any of my sisters."

"Thank you, dearest." Bingley kissed her hand repeatedly. "You are too good. Other women would not tolerate such a sudden departure of the betrothed only a few weeks before the wedding."

Jane smiled bravely. "Let us hope that Caroline's health will improve enough so that she can attend the ceremony."

"Miss Bingley will not be present at my wedding," Darcy, who had been silent so far, announced.

"We cannot know that, Mr. Darcy," Jane countered gently. "She may feel well enough to participate."

"I wish her rapid return to health. However, I do not look forward to seeing her again anytime soon," Darcy responded coldly, his eyes narrowed. "I will not allow her near Elizabeth or my sister."

"Is that not too harsh?" Jane enquired.

Darcy shook his head. "No, it is not. Caroline Bingley assaulted Elizabeth. If I had not been standing close by, I cannot even imagine how it would have ended."

"I do not blame you, Darcy," Mr. Bingley supported him. "Even if Caroline's condition improves enough for her to be in the company again, I do not believe that she should attend our wedding."

"It is settled, then," Darcy said, raising to his feet and walking to stand by the window.

"Miss Elizabeth," Bingley said, turning his attention to his future sister. "I cannot express how deeply sorry I am for the distress that you experienced last evening. It was my mistake that I had not informed my sister about your engagement to

Darcy earlier on. In my defence, though, I was convinced that she had already heard about it."

"It is not your fault, Mr. Bingley," Elizabeth assured him graciously. "No one could have predicted the events of last evening, not even Caroline, I believe."

"I do not understand Caroline's fixation," Darcy spoke from his spot by the window. "I have never done anything to encourage her affection."

"I think that it is her own imagination that is her worst enemy," Elizabeth observed. "She allowed herself to believe in something which only existed in her own head."

"When are you leaving London?" Jane asked, her eyes on Bingley.

"The day after tomorrow," he responded, kissing her hand again.

They did not speak more on the subject of Miss Bingley or Bingley's departure because the little Gardiners entered the drawing room together with their mother. The gentlemen were asked to stay for dinner, but only Darcy accepted the invitation. Bingley excused himself, explaining that he needed to make preparations for the journey.

Elizabeth felt deeply for her sister's misfortune. Jane was to spend the weeks before her wedding away from her betrothed. Elizabeth did not care much for Caroline. However, for Jane's sake, she hoped that Miss Bingley returned to full health soon.

Jane had no need for such complications at the onset of her married life.

***

Mrs. Bennet was most displeased when the news of Mr. Bingley's departure from London reached her. She was suspicious of Miss Bingley's sudden and mysterious illness, guessing that it was another plot to separate Bingley from Jane.

"I do not understand why Mr. Bingley needs to stay in there with her?" she asked loudly the day after the Bingleys left for Ramsgate.

"She is seriously ill, Mama," Jane reminded her for the tenth time. "She needs care."

"She has a sister, I believe. What about her? Is it not her duty to take care of her younger sibling in the hour of need?"

"Mrs. Hurst is with child," Elizabeth explained.

"And the aunt from Scarborough? Cannot she take her?"

"The relatives from Scarborough refused to host Caroline anymore," Darcy said. "There was no one to keep her company but Charles."

Mrs. Bennet was still not convinced. "If she is so ill, she needs physicians and nurses, not her brother. Mr. Bingley should have hired help to assist his sister in Ramsgate. He should be here with Jane."

"Mama, I do understand why Mr. Bingley had to go, and I support him," Jane announced.

"Oh, Jane, my dear, I am only afraid that Miss Bingley wants to put distance between you and our dear Mr. Bingley. What if she tries to prevent him from leaving her side in time for your wedding?"

Mrs. Bennet waved her hand in front of her face, visibly distressed. "Oh, my poor, poor nerves! I cannot think calmly about this situation. Why is it happening to us? I do not like it. I simply do not like it. And I do not trust Caroline Bingley! From the very beginning she has looked down upon us, thinking herself to be something better."

"Do not fret, Madam," Darcy spoke then. "I will bring Bingley in front of the altar from Ramsgate by myself if necessary. My dearest Elizabeth wishes to marry the same day as her most beloved sister, and not even Caroline Bingley can prevent it."

+++

"Mama was very much impressed with your promise to bring Mr. Bingley back in time for the wedding," Elizabeth said the next day as they were strolling the grounds of Vauxhall Gardens.

"I did not say that to please your mother."

"Nevertheless, you calmed her with your assurances."

"I will not allow Caroline Bingley to ruin our wedding day."

"Do you agree with Mama that she is not truly ill and that she is trying to manipulate Mr. Bingley for her own benefit?"

"I think that she was truly not in her right mind that evening when she tried to attack you. There was something in her eyes and voice which could not be faked unless she were an excellent performer, which I doubt. However, I fear that your mother is indeed right and that she will try to influence Bingley once she feels better."

"Poor Jane. It should be one of the happiest times of her life."

"I agree. Your sister does not deserve to be separated from Bingley now. I can only hope that Caroline will realise soon that for her own good she should accept Jane and support Charles in his marriage."

"I think that Caroline hates me."

Darcy looked down at her with great concern. "You do not have to fear her, my dearest. I will protect you from her; you can trust me on this. You will never have to see her again. "

"I am not afraid of Caroline; I simply cannot imagine our future relationship," she responded. "We will belong to one family; you and Bingley will be brothers, Jane and Caroline sisters. Family gatherings cannot be avoided."

"It is Charles's problem, not ours," Darcy spoke confidently. "He cannot forbid her from his house, I imagine, but we surely can refuse to host her at Pemberley after what happened. She will be persona non grata, just like Wickham. Caroline Bingley has proved to us that she cannot be trusted."

Their conversation was interrupted by the arrival of three little Gardiners, who ran towards them with great speed as fast as their short legs allowed them. Their youngest brother was sick to his stomach, and Darcy had offered to take the rest of the brood on a trip, wishing to give Mrs. Gardiner some rest.

Elizabeth was greatly touched with Darcy's thoughtfulness. He must have noticed how tired Mrs. Gardiner looked this morning after a mostly sleepless night. Although there were not many attractions left in the Vauxhall Gardens at this time of the year, the children were entertained enough by running around and looking at the various sights. The day away from home and everyday routine was a grand attraction for them on its own.

As they approached the stand with food and drinks, Darcy bought roasted chestnuts and gingerbread for the children. With the little mouths and hands occupied for several minutes, Elizabeth and Darcy were allowed to carry on with their conversation.

"I am immensely sorry that your stay in London began with such an unfortunate event," he spoke. "I imagined it quite differently, I assure you."

"As it has been said before many times, no one could have foreseen such behaviour on Caroline's part. Jane is the one who suffered the most as a result of it."

"We should involve Miss Jane on our outings and company

on a regular basis."

Elizabeth shook her head. "She will not want to impose."

"Then we should invite your mother to my townhouse for the rest of your stay in town. This way it would be easier to include Miss Jane in our daily activities. Bingley asked me to take care of her during his absence."

Elizabeth stopped walking, staring at him with her eyes wide open. "Have I heard you correctly?" she asked after a long minute of muteness. "You wish to invite Mama to your home to live there?"

He nodded. "Together with you and Jane, naturally. I do believe that the Gardiners feel burdened with such a large company gathered at their house, which often includes not only Bingley and I, but also Georgiana. They are too polite to say anything, but their house is simply too small. Your mother and Jane will be much more comfortable in my...in our house," he corrected himself quickly.

"Mama will be delighted."

"It is settled, then."

Elizabeth resumed her walk, marvelling again at the goodness of the man by her side. She knew that Darcy merely tolerated her mother, but still he was ready to welcome her in his house even though he did not have to. "Thank you, Fitzwilliam," she said, reaching her hand to squeeze his gloved hand.

Looking warmly at her, he smiled, squinting his eyes. "My reasons for inviting your family may be quite selfish. Has it not occurred to you?"

Elizabeth opened her mouth but then closed it, saying nothing. She smiled secretly. Even with the presence of her mother and sister, they would be under the same roof, creating more opportunity for privacy.

CHAPTER TEN

Elizabeth was busy packing her and Jane's dresses into the trunk when Mrs. Gardiner walked into the room.

"I hope, Lizzy, that you do not feel obliged to leave our home before the end of your stay in London."

"Dear Aunt, I know that we are always welcome here. However, I am also aware that Mama can be a bit demanding, and you have enough on your hands with four small children as well as this one." Elizabeth placed her hand on the other woman's burgeoning midsection. "It the baby kicking?"

"Yes, but much less than the previous ones. He or she will be a calm one, I hope," Mrs. Gardiner answered. She removed an abandoned bonnet from a chair before sitting on it. "Your mother is delighted with Mr. Darcy's invitation."

Elizabeth rolled her eyes. "To say the least. I can only hope that Mama will be able to restrain herself once she is at Darcy's townhouse. I fear that she will begin to order the servants around and count the silvers."

"Do not fret yourself so much about your mother, Lizzy. I think that Mr. Darcy knows her character well enough by now not to be further surprised."

"He seems to tolerate her rather well."

"He simply loves you very much."

Elizabeth smiled. "And I do love him. Darcy likes you and Uncle Edward very much indeed."

"The feeling is mutual, Lizzy. We both hold him in very high esteem. I cannot imagine a better man for you."

"I was so pleased that I could introduce both of you to him when we toured Derbyshire. I wanted to prove to him that I had relatives who are cultured, worldly and well mannered. Someone that I did not need to be ashamed of."

"Lizzy..." Mrs. Gardiner began with hesitation in her voice.

"Yes, Aunt?" Elizabeth asked, occupied with folding another layer of dresses, thinking that even after a few hours in the trunk they would be quite creased and would need to be pressed again.

"Do not think that I wish to prey into your personal life. However, I must admit that I am quite curious about one matter."

Elizabeth's dark green eyes rested on her aunt with attention. "You can ask me anything, but I cannot promise to answer," she answered with a teasing smile.

"Were you aware that Darcy was in love with you at the time we were touring Derbyshire?"

Elizabeth considered her answer for a moment. "I knew that he had loved me once, but I was quite certain that he hated me at the time of our trip."

"Hated you?" Mrs. Gardiner enquired disbelievingly.

"Yes. After my refusal of his first marriage proposal, I had no doubt that his love for me must have turned into dislike, or something even stronger than that."

Mrs. Gardiner sat silently for a moment longer while Elizabeth finished packing the bonnets, careful to put them in boxes in a way that would not ruin them.

"May I ask when did he propose?"

"Last April."

"At the time you were visiting Charlotte Lucas?"

"Yes. He was in Kent for a few weeks to see his aunt at Rosings Park."

Elizabeth closed the trunk and looked around the room, wondering whether she had forgotten something. If she had, they would put it into the larger carpet bag which Jane had brought with herself from home.

She sat on the edge of the bed, resting her gaze on her aunt, who still looked as if she could not believe what she had just heard. "Will you not ask why I refused him?"

"I am certain that you had very good reasons, Lizzy," Mrs. Gardiner spoke quickly.

"At the time I certainly thought that I had them," Elizabeth agreed.

Mrs. Bennet entered the room, putting an end to further conversation. Mrs. Gardiner did not have to be told not to discuss certain matters in front of her sister-in-law. She was well aware that both Jane and Elizabeth never confessed any secrets to their mother.

"Are you packed, Lizzy?" Mrs. Bennet asked.

"I believe so, Mama. I think that I took everything that I should have."

"If not, we can always send what was left in the following days," Mrs. Gardiner said. "Mayfair is not that far away, after all."

Mrs. Bennet walked to her brother's wife, standing by her side. "I do hope, Maddie, that you are not offended with our departure."

"Not at all, Sister. I will miss your company, though."

Mrs. Bennet straightened, lifting her chin proudly. "Well, you must understand that we could not refuse Mr. Darcy's kind offer."

Mrs. Gardiner looked over at Elizabeth, winking at her. "Of course you could not. You will visit us before your return to Longbourn. I wish to see you often for the rest of your stay in London, as I will not be able to attend Lizzy's wedding."

Mrs. Bennet promised to visit at least twice a week. Next, the conversation settled on the subject of the date of the arrival of the newest addition to the Gardiner family. Mrs. Gardiner was certain that it would be the first day of February, while Mrs. Bennet tried to convince her that the middle of January was more probable. Elizabeth barely restrained herself from rolling her eyes at her mother's persistence as to the date of the birth of her niece or nephew. After all, her aunt knew best how far along she was in her condition, especially so since it was her fifth child.

***

"And this will be your room," Darcy said as they entered a light green bedroom.

"It is lovely," Elizabeth assured, looking around.

"I thought that you would prefer the one with the view over the backyard rather than the street."

She stepped to one of the tall windows and looked out. The long strip of grass was narrow, the exact width of the house, but it was long, and neatly connected with the neighbouring gardens. She did not expect so much of greenery in the middle of London, especially as her only point of reference was a small garden belonging to the Gardiners' house in Cheapside.

Darcy came to stand behind her. "It is not Pemberley, for sure."

Elizabeth turned to face him, sitting on the windowsill with her back to the glass. "You dislike the town," she stated.

"Dislike is too strong a word. I simply prefer the country. I cannot imagine living in London all year long."

"You would prefer to stay at Pemberley all year long."

"I would. Since I was a boy, my father encouraged me to

work at the stables with the horses, also with cattle, sheep, and in the fields at the harvest. I will do the same with our sons. It will help them value the privileges but also understand the responsibilities that come from being a Darcy. I do enjoy manual labour even now. It helps to take my mind away from worries. After last April I spent long weeks working as no more than a stable hand. I thought it would help me to forget you."

Elizabeth reached for his hand, opening his palm, examining his long fingers, looking for confirmation to his words. It was not a hand of someone who had never known manual labour; on the contrary, it was strong and calloused in places. "Did it help?"

He smiled. "No, but it served its purpose. By the end of the day I was so tired that I could sleep all night without recurring dreams of you."

Standing up, she stood close to him, placing his hand on her waist. "You promised me something back at Netherfield."

It did not take long for him to understand her meaning, and answer, "I do not remember promising you anything. I said only that I would try to find some private time for us."

"Then try."

The tone of his voice dropped as he spoke. "I do not wish for your mother to suspect that I invited you here only to have my way with you."

"You know very well that my mother would be the least upset if she suspected anything of the kind."

"Elizabeth, dearest." He enclosed her in his arms, looking into her eyes. "'Tis only a few weeks until our wedding."

"Five," she clarified.

"In a little over a month we shall be together at Pemberley, and I promise you that we will not leave our bedchamber for three days or more."

Elizabeth rose on her toes, supporting her hands on his broad arms, and pressed her lips to his. He responded to the kiss with mild ardour, but all too soon he ended it gently but decidedly.

"I beg you to cease this, Elizabeth. It is a torture to kiss and hold you like this, but not be able to fully consummate our union. We must restrain ourselves until our wedding."

Elizabeth frowned, stepping away from him. "I understand you perfectly well, sir. I will forbid myself from imposing my person on you furthermore."

"Do not be cross with me, darling." He lifted her hand to his lips.

She freed her hand from his hold and smoothed down her skirts. "Let us return to the drawing room. Mama and Jane are surely waiting for us with tea."

"Elizabeth," he said with longing in his voice, but she ignored him, hurrying out of the room.

***

The next few days proved to be so busy for Elizabeth that even if Darcy had showed more willingness, it would have been difficult to find time to see each other for more than a quarter of an hour. Mrs. Bennet insisted on meeting with the seamstresses every day so that Elizabeth and Jane's new wardrobes were finished on time. Moreover, looking for the right kind of accessories such as gloves, hats, shawls, and reticules that matched the new outfits was also consuming a lot of time.

Darcy suggested that Elizabeth should speak with the housekeeper at the townhouse. They would not return to London until later next year. In his view it was a good opportunity for Elizabeth to begin dealing with her new duties as Mrs. Darcy. As it was expected, Mrs. Bennet supported Darcy wholeheartedly, practically ordering her daughter to summon the housekeeper and look over the household accounts with her. Elizabeth was astonished, though, that her mother did not wish to join her in order to advise her. Mrs. Bennet stated that Elizabeth had to deal with it on her own.

"Once in Derbyshire, there will be no one to help you. Remember what I taught you and your sisters in that respect. You are a clever girl, Lizzy, and you will do just fine."

That was perhaps the highest praise that Elizabeth had ever received from her mother in her life.

The days passed quickly, November turning into December. Jane received long letters from Mr. Bingley almost every day, and it seemed that the gentleman did nothing more in Ramsgate but write, or rather scribble, to his lady, because the letters were long but also at times difficult to read. Jane asked Elizabeth a few times to help her to decipher them. The news, however, were not good. Caroline was calm and quiet but also very sad. She barely spoke to anyone and ate very little. She was reluctant to leave the house, even though the physician recommended long walks and other outdoor activities like horse riding.

Elizabeth felt for poor Mr. Bingley, who was a good man, for not wishing to leave his sister in the hour of need. At the same time she was upset with Caroline's behaviour, feeling that the woman was trying to separate Bingley from Jane. She did not doubt Caroline's illness, but she also did not trust her in the least.

Her only consolation in the matter was that Darcy had promised to her that he would bring Bingley to Netherfield in time for the wedding.

***

Elizabeth walked into her sister's bedroom without knocking, as the door was open.

"Lizzy, will you help me with this?" Jane asked, trying to push the loose curl which fell out of her coiffure.

"Darcy told me earlier that you received a letter from Mr. Bingley," Elizabeth said, pushing two pins into her sister's pale blonde hair to secure any wayward locks from escaping.

"I did. Charles wrote that Caroline's condition has not changed. She seems indifferent to what is happening around her."

"She is not indifferent to the fact that her brother sits with her instead of being here with you."

"Lizzy, do not be unkind. Caroline is sick."

"Caroline is spoiled."

"Charles is afraid that she will attempt to harm herself if he leaves her alone too soon."

Elizabeth put her arms around her sister, hugging her, careful not to ruin the hairstyle. "Oh, Jane. I cannot imagine ever being as good as you are. I could not be so considerate and patient in your place."

"Imagine Georgiana being sick. Would you forbid Mr. Darcy from taking care of her?"

"Of course not."

"There, you see?"

"There is a considerable difference. Georgiana is very much different than Caroline. She would never try to use her illness to manipulate her brother."

"I believe that Caroline is not as bad as you perceive her, Lizzy. She is lost and confused in her beliefs, views, and general understanding of the world. She is not happy with her own company, which makes her miserable. But let us talk about something different. I must say that I am pleased that Colonel Fitzwilliam is joining us tonight. I am quite curious about him. Georgiana speaks so highly of him."

"Colonel Fitzwilliam is a very engaging companion. I am also looking forward to this evening. Even more so now that the Gardiners are coming," Elizabeth informed.

"They are?"

"Mama told me that she received a message from Uncle. Aunt feels restless at home and he convinced her to accept Darcy's invitation for the dinner."

"It was good of Mr. Darcy to include the Gardiners."

Elizabeth nodded. "He is genuinely fond of them. He said to me that he would always be grateful to them that they brought me to Derbyshire instead of travelling farther on to the Lake District."

***

Elizabeth watched in great amusement Colonel Fitzwilliam's expression as he was introduced to her elder sister. The gentleman lost the power of speech for a moment, simply staring. It was an expected reaction to Jane's beauty, one Elizabeth had witnessed many times before.

"Your sister is very beautiful," Colonel Fitzwilliam told her himself later on as they were waiting for dinner to be served.

"She is. I have never seen anyone more beautiful."

Colonel Fitzwilliam looked at her in wonder. "You are not jealous of her beauty," he stated.

"I am not. I have never been. Jane is the sweetest and kindest person in the world. I love her; I cannot imagine being jealous of her. I am proud that she is admired wherever she goes."

"She seems very kind," Colonel Fitzwilliam agreed. "I cannot believe that my foolish cousin tried to talk Bingley out of marrying her."

Elizabeth's eyes widened. "You knew that it was my sister?"

"At the time we spoke during our walk in Rosings Park?" he guessed her thought. "No, I did not know. It was simply a piece of gossip I repeated to you. Darcy made me realize the identity of the lady in question a few weeks later. Had I known that it was your sister, I would have never..."

"It does not matter now, Colonel Fitzwilliam. Both Jane and I are very happy."

"Still, it was a lesson for me to watch my tongue next time."

Elizabeth smiled at him graciously, hoping to reassure him that she held no ill feelings towards him.

"May I say how pleased I am that the matter between Darcy and you has been resolved so well?"

"Thank you."

"He is very happy. I have never seen him so; perhaps only

when his mother still lived."

"I hope to maintain his state of happiness."

Colonel Fitzwilliam leaned towards her, saying, "And I am certain that you will be successful in your endeavour."

The way he said the words and looked at her made Elizabeth blush a little. She suddenly remembered that there was a time when she had regretted that Colonel Fitzwilliam had no means to be seriously interested in her.

"You told me that you learned that it was my sister of whom we talked about that afternoon in Kent a few weeks later," she said, hoping to hear more about it.

"Yes, indeed. It was at the end of May, I believe. Darcy was behaving strangely. He was very upset upon leaving Kent, and he did it so abruptly. Then he did not reply to any of my letters. When I was on my way to Matlock to visit my parents, I decided to pay him a visit at Pemberley. I was worried that he was sick."

Elizabeth watched his face closely, waiting for him to continue.

Colonel Fitzwilliam cleared his throat. "I know that you had good reasons to refuse Darcy, and I daresay that this experience taught him a lot, but I would not wish to see him ever again in the state that he was at the time."

Some invisible string tugged at Elizabeth's heart. "I am truly sorry to hear that."

"But as I have said, it did him good in the end. He is an excellent man, the best—however, he needs guidance on occasion, like any of us."

Dinner was announced, interrupting their conversation. Elizabeth looked around, searching for Darcy to accompany her to the dining room, but he had already offered his arm to Mrs. Gardiner. Elizabeth was left to be escorted by Colonel Fitzwilliam.

The meal was excellent, and everyone seemed to enjoy it. Elizabeth praised herself silently at choosing the right menu. She was enjoying the excellent soup when Mrs. Gardiner, who sat on her right side, leaned towards her, speaking quietly, "Lizzy, I would be more careful in your place."

"Careful?"

"Mr. Darcy was not pleased when you talked with his cousin for so long."

"But we discussed Darcy himself," Elizabeth protested.

Mrs. Gardiner looked her right in the eye. "You smiled at Colonel Fitzwilliam, and seemed very pleased with his company."

Elizabeth looked over at Darcy, who was staring at his plate, a heavy frown settled on his forehead.

"Colonel Fitzwilliam is not only Darcy's cousin, but also his best friend. Darcy trusts him more than anyone else in the world. He trusts him with Georgiana."

"It does not mean, however, that he enjoys watching you flirting with him," Mrs. Gardiner cut her short.

Elizabeth opened her mouth to deny such allegations but then closed it. She was glad to see Colonel Fitzwilliam. He was easy company. Was she flirting with him, though?

CHAPTER ELEVEN

The following day, Elizabeth was ready to agree with her aunt that she had been right yesterday saying that Darcy was jealous of Colonel Fitzwilliam.

Darcy was reserved and quiet, even more than usual. He did not seek her company. He was avoiding her, closing himself in his study for long hours. He was polite but also distant. They were to leave for Hertfordshire in three days, and the initial plan was that Darcy and Georgiana were to travel with them. However, now Darcy said that he would have to stay in town for a few more days and only Georgiana would join the Bennet ladies.

Elizabeth could not believe that her short conversation with Colonel Fitzwilliam could have caused such a change in him.

When he chose to take tea alone in his study the second time in two days, Elizabeth decided that she had to address the matter, as this behaviour could not last any longer.

She excused herself to her mother, Jane and Georgiana, explaining that she would join Darcy for tea.

"I thought that you might wish for company," she announced with a smile, entering the library, the maid following her with a tray with tea and refreshments.

Darcy put away a letter that he was reading and stood up to greet her. "It would be my pleasure," he assured, but his voice and manner were guarded.

Elizabeth sent the maid away, fixing him a cup the way he liked it with sugar but without milk.

They enjoyed tea in silence for some time before she asked, "Fitzwilliam, are you upset with me?"

He put down his empty cup and said nothing.

"Fitzwilliam," she probed.

"I am not upset, Elizabeth. I simply realized something in the course of the last few days."

"Oh? What is it?"

He shrugged his broad shoulders, looking down at his hands. "Nothing of importance. Will you leave me now? I still have much correspondence to attend to."

"Fitzwilliam," she repeated.

He looked her right in the eye. "What do you want from me, Elizabeth?"

"Talk to me."

"There is nothing to talk about. Please join your mother and our sisters. I wish to complete as many matters as possible before the wedding."

Darcy returned to the desk, sitting down in the leather chair and opening the letter which he had been reading before she had come.

Elizabeth knew that he had dismissed her, but she was not one to admit defeat easily. She came to stand beside his chair, placing her hand on his shoulder. "Are you upset about me conversing with Colonel Fitzwilliam?"

He stiffened visibly under her touch, not tearing his eyes away from his letter. "You showed your preference very clearly that evening, madam."

"Fitzwilliam," she pleaded, cupping his cheek, forcing him to look at her. "We spoke about you."

He searched her eyes. "Did you?"

"You can ask him if you do not believe me."

"I will not ask him anything. I made a fool of myself in front of him too many times for my liking."

Elizabeth felt that his formidable pride was coming to voice. She knew that it was a dangerous opponent, even to her. Leaning down, she kissed his lips, stroking his cheek. "I love you."

"I love you too," he answered, his tone flat. "Now go, join the other ladies. I truly have much correspondence to attend to."

Elizabeth stepped back with a sigh. She did not know how to convince him that the conversation that she had with Colonel Fitzwilliam meant nothing to her. "Shall I see you at dinner?"

"Of course," he answered, not looking at her.

She left the room, not liking in the least the feeling of

rejection overpowering her.

***

It was their last evening in London. Jane and Elizabeth decided to spend it dining with the Gardiners at their home in Cheapside. Mrs. Bennet declined to join them, announcing that she had to rest before tomorrow's journey to Hertfordshire. Elizabeth was not quite certain that leaving Darcy and her mother alone for even a few hours was a sound idea. However, Jane pointed out to her that they did not have to sit in the same room. If Mrs. Bennet was indeed tired, she would want to dine alone in her bedroom.

As always when entering the Gardiners' house, Elizabeth felt warmth envelop her heart. Mr. Gardiner was sitting near the fireplace with his two youngest children draped over him, and the two older ones playing at his feet. Mrs. Gardiner was settled in her favourite armchair, looking at fashion illustrations from "Lady's Magazine," planning the dresses that she would wear after regaining her figure.

"If I had my way, this one would be my last one," she said, touching her belly as Jane and Elizabeth sat next to her.

"You are tired, dear Aunt," Jane guessed.

"I feel restless. What I dislike most is being trapped in a house for so many months every time. I cannot bear that I will not be able to attend the wedding of my two beloved nieces."

"You still can," Elizabeth insisted. "The child will not be

born earlier than January, you said it yourself."

"Your uncle is against me travelling when I am so far along in my condition. I should not be seen in public, people will gossip. It is different to attend a dinner at a private house than a wedding."

"We were selfish in setting the wedding date so early," Jane said. "We should have taken into consideration that you would not be able to attend. A spring wedding would be lovely as well, do you not agree, Lizzy?"

"I am afraid that Mr. Darcy would not be pleased with a spring wedding," Elizabeth noted. "He thinks those three months of engagement to be too long already."

Mrs. Gardiner smiled. "Do not concern yourself with me. I still remember how it was to be young and in love. Your uncle and I did not have a long engagement either. Once I was certain of my feelings, I did not wish to wait even a week longer than necessary."

"We do hope that you will come to Pemberley for the entire summer," Elizabeth said. "The children will love it there."

"Oh, I know that they would. However, I am not certain whether Mr. Darcy will be happy to house all seven of us."

"He mentioned it to me himself," Elizabeth insisted. "He may not express himself in so many words, but he truly wishes you to come."

"Lizzy is right," Jane supported her. "Mr. Darcy likes you the most out of all our family. Papa is his second favourite, I believe."

"There is a friendship between Mr. Darcy and your father, Lizzy?" Mrs. Gardiner enquired, looking curiously at Elizabeth.

"'Friendship' is too strong a word, for now at least. They do not mind each other. They can sit in the library together for hours, each occupied with a book, speaking barely a few words."

"I see." The older woman nodded.

"Jane received a letter from Mr. Bingley today," Elizabeth said.

Mrs. Gardiner sent her elder niece a look full of concern. "How is his sister?"

Jane sighed. "Her condition is not improving."

"Aunt, do you not agree that it is truly terrible that Jane is separated from Mr. Bingley only a few weeks before their wedding?"

"It is not an ideal situation, for sure. However, what else can be done? Mr. Bingley is a good man. He cannot abandon his sister in her hour of need, even if it does not suit his own plans."

"Lizzy is of opinion that Caroline is not as ill as we think," Jane mentioned.

Mrs. Gardiner seemed sincerely surprised with such an allegation. "Truly, Lizzy?"

"I suspect that she wishes to separate Jane and her brother. She did it once before, last year. I simply do not trust her."

"You believe that she is manipulating Mr. Bingley into believing that her condition is worse than it truly is?"

Elizabeth nodded. "Exactly."

"What is your opinion, Aunt?" Jane enquired. "I do not wish to believe that Caroline would do such a thing."

"Well, Jane, we have to remember that Miss Bingley is capable of deceit, of which we have the best proof in her behaviour from last winter when she hid from her brother your presence in London."

"Exactly," Elizabeth repeated.

"Still, we should not forget the way she acted that evening at Darcy's townhouse when she realized that Mr. Darcy and Lizzy were engaged. We all witnessed her distress, and I refuse to believe that she pretended it. She truly was unwell, completely losing control over herself."

"The only good news is that Mr. Darcy vowed to travel to Ramsgate himself in order to bring Mr. Bingley in time for the wedding, no matter what condition he found Caroline in."

"Darcy is a man of his word. If he indeed said that to you, Lizzy, there is no doubt that he will keep his promise," Mrs. Gardiner announced with authority.

The little Gardiners ran to Jane and Elizabeth, demanding their participation in their game of hide-and-seek, for which they had failed to recruit their father. Jane volunteered to play with them, seeing that Elizabeth preferred to stay in their aunt's company.

"Well, then, Lizzy, how are your spirits?" Mrs. Gardiner asked, smiling at the younger woman. "In three weeks you will be a married woman. Nervous?"

"I am anticipating it but at the same time I feel overwhelmed. I cannot sleep at night even though I am tired, especially on days when Mama insists on visiting every single shop in town to find the perfect shade of gloves to match a bonnet. Only two months ago I thought that Mr. Darcy would be gone from my life forever, that I would perhaps see him at Jane's wedding."

"It is most fortunate that you and Mr. Darcy found each other again, explained all your differences."

"Yes, it is."

Mrs. Gardiner peered at her closely. "Forgive me, Lizzy, but you do seem a bit subdued to me tonight. Are you worrying over your new role as the mistress of the grand estate?"

Elizabeth shook her head. "I will try my very best to fulfil my new duties. I feel that Mama prepared us well in that respect. Moreover, I believe that I learnt a lot observing you during many visits here over the years. Being Mistress of Pemberley is a challenge that will welcome."

"Are you concerned about the more intimate side of the

marriage?"

Elizabeth blinked in surprise at her aunt's directness. "No, of course not," she answered without hesitation.

"No?"

"Mr. Darcy is very gentlemanlike in that respect."

"He is? How can you know?"

"He has barely touched me since our engagement."

"I see."

"I have tried to entice him, but..."

Mrs. Gardiner smiled knowingly. "You have?"

Elizabeth sighed. "He claims that we should wait, that there is a time and place for everything, that we should restrain ourselves until after the wedding."

"You do not agree with him."

"It is of no importance now because he is so displeased with me that I do not believe that he will even kiss me goodbye tomorrow."

Mrs. Gardiner touched her hand. "What happened, Lizzy?"

Elizabeth rolled her eyes. "He is jealous of Colonel Fitzwilliam."

"I cannot say that I am surprised. He said that to you?"

"When I asked him about it, he said that I had showed my true preference that evening when Colonel Fitzwilliam dined with us."

"It is a lesson for you, Elizabeth," Mrs. Gardiner told her

sternly.

"I still do not understand what I did wrong. Colonel Fitzwilliam and I talked about Darcy. We were not flirting."

"Were you not?"

"Dear Aunt, you too?" Elizabeth asked with hurt in her voice.

"If I noticed how comfortable you were around Colonel Fitzwilliam, I am certain that Darcy felt it ten times as much," Mrs. Gardiner lectured. "Mr. Darcy was once rejected by you, remember? He knows that you disliked him once; also, he is intelligent enough to realize that you changed your opinion about him largely because he helped your youngest sister and rescued your family's reputation. You cannot blame him that he may be a bit insecure about his feelings towards you."

"I assured him that I loved him."

"I do not doubt that he believes you, but when he saw you with his cousin, conversing so animatedly, he might have thought that if the circumstances were different, you would have chosen Colonel Fitzwilliam over him."

"It is a gross untruth. I like Colonel Fitzwilliam's company. However, I have never been in love with him."

"I only try to present to you the way Mr. Darcy sees it."

"It is ridiculous," Elizabeth argued. "It seems that now I cannot even talk to and smile at other gentlemen."

"Unless the gentleman in question is your father or uncle, I would advise not, at least until you and Mr. Darcy feel more secure in your marriage. Imagine, Lizzy, how you would feel if Mr. Darcy spent the entire evening in the company of a young, attractive woman, ignoring you entirely."

"I was not ignoring him!" Elizabeth exclaimed loudly, drawing the attention of Mr. Gardiner, who was currently supervising the building process of a castle made of wooden blocks. "I was not ignoring him," Elizabeth repeated in a whisper, her expression determined.

"You are defending yourself too much for my taste, my dear."

Elizabeth sat quietly for a moment longer, considering Mrs. Gardiner's words and her own feelings. Her aunt had a point when she observed that she would not be pleased to watch Darcy laughing with some other single woman right in front of her eyes.

"What should I do now?" she asked. "How to convince him of my devotion?"

"Mr. Darcy needs time, I believe. In a few days he will hopefully forget about it."

"Hopefully? He is not returning with us tomorrow," Elizabeth complained. "He claims that he needs to stay in London for a couple of days to finalize all his business."

"Perhaps it is not such a bad idea. Not seeing you for some time, he will begin to miss your company and it will be easier for him to put this matter to rest."

"I do hope so, as I do not know what to say to convince him that his cousin is of no consequence to me."

"Such matters need time. Marriage is the union of two minds, two bodies, two characters. There will be times when you will see things differently. The most important thing is to remember to mind the other person's needs and feelings, at the same time not forgetting about your own."

"For the last year I have known Mr. Darcy, we rarely saw eye to eye. It does not bode well for our marriage."

Mrs. Gardiner put her arm around Elizabeth, hugging her. "Oh, Lizzy, you and Mr. Darcy will do just fine. I know that you will do your very best to succeed in this new endeavour. You have the example of your parents' union, and I do not believe that you wish to repeat their mistakes."

"I do not," Elizabeth confirmed with determination.

Mrs. Gardiner smiled. "I know. Your Mr. Darcy is an excellent man. You will have a good life together."

CHAPTER TWELVE

"Then there will be forty-five guests at the wedding breakfast," Mrs. Bennet said as she frowned over the list she had scribbled on a single sheet of paper.

"Is it not too many, Mama?" Jane asked.

"Too many!" her mother exclaimed. "Not at all! I would gladly invite more if we only had a larger house."

Elizabeth sat with a book, curled in the window seat, absentmindedly listening to the chatter of her family, trying to read at the same time.

She was glad that her mother and Jane took over the wedding preparations. After weeks in London filled with time-consuming and tedious visits to the seamstresses and shoe and hat shops, she welcomed their return to Longbourn with quiet relief. Her time was her own, as Darcy was still in London. She was free to take long walks and enjoy her own company, even though the weather was cold and more suited to sitting by the mantelpiece in a warm home rather than being outdoors.

She was glad to see her father, and they spent long hours in the library. They discussed books as well as current affairs, avoiding the topic of her impending marriage. Soon they would be separated for many months, perhaps even a year.

Darcy was not keen on leaving Pemberley in the near future. Countless times he had mentioned to her how pleased he was that at last he would be able to stay in his ancestral home for a longer time in the upcoming year.

Mr. Bennet began to fully comprehend that soon two of his most liked and intelligent daughters would leave his home. At least Jane would live close by, but Elizabeth, the only person in his household that could hold a sensible conversation about literature, history, and poetry, would live in the far north. Darcy was not a man who would wish to be separate from his wife for longer periods of time, especially so early in the marriage. Mr. Bennet tried to improve his own mood, already planning a trip to Pemberley and its famous library. He hoped that in March, once the roads were drier, it would not be too soon to visit the newlyweds. He also thought hard about how to discourage his wife and younger daughters from joining him. It would not be an easy task.

"When is Mr. Darcy returning, Lizzy?" Mrs. Bennet asked, demanding Elizabeth's attention.

"Any day now, Mama," Elizabeth answered calmly.

"You said that yesterday and the day before," the older woman accused. "Are you certain that Mr. Darcy is not cross with you over something? Did you say something to him that might have offended him? I told you before that your teasing is good between friends and family, but Mr. Darcy will be your husband and you should have more respect for him."

"Mr. Darcy is a very busy man, Mama," Jane reminded her. "He has many responsibilities to attend to. You remember how Uncle Gardiner told us that Mr. Darcy was interested in investing in his business."

Mrs. Bennet sighed, her expression most unhappy. "I simply cannot understand why two weeks before the wedding both of my future sons are so far away from my daughters!" she exclaimed, fanning herself with her hand. "Oh, my poor nerves! What a year it has been! Three daughters married! I will not leave my room a week after it all ends."

Elizabeth and Jane exchanged knowing looks. They had no doubt that the second day after the wedding their mother would be visiting her friends, informing them about all the details from the ceremony and the wedding breakfast that might have skipped their attention.

Elizabeth returned to her book, but was only able to read a few pages when Mrs. Bennet demanded her attention again.

"Have you unpacked those dresses which arrived from London yesterday, Lizzy?"

"No, I haven't, Mama."

Mrs. Bennet's eyes widened dramatically. "Why ever not?"

Elizabeth shrugged. "I did not see the point. They are summer dresses, much too thin to wear them now. I will simply put them in my trunk when the time comes to pack it for our trip to Derbyshire."

"Are you not curious how they turned out, Lizzy?" Jane asked.

"I already saw them during the last visit with the seamstress."

"You see, Jane, what I have to suffer with this girl?" Mrs. Bennet complained. "I cannot believe her! Such beautiful dresses and she will not even look at them! You should be thankful that Mr. Darcy was so generous to pay for all those fine things that we were able to purchase in London. Any other girl would be trying them on and admiring them for long hours."

Elizabeth rolled her eyes.

Her mother pointed her finger at her. "I saw that, Elizabeth Bennet. Do not roll your eyes at me! I am your mother! I hope that you are not so insolent when in the company of Mr. Darcy."

Jane smiled. "I think, Mama, that Mr. Darcy likes the fact that Elizabeth does not always agree with him. He quite likes her teasing manner."

"But I am certain that he would not tolerate rudeness." Mrs. Bennet clutched her generous bosom where her heart was and exclaimed, "Oh, my poor nerves! I doubt that my heart will survive all this worry."

"Why should you be worried, Mama?" Jane asked reasonably. "After all, you succeeded in marrying three out of five daughters. It has always been your biggest concern to find good husbands for all of us."

"Almost, dear Jane, almost married," Mrs. Bennet stressed. "Who knows what will happen in the next two weeks? Mr. Darcy is in London, while Mr. Bingley stays in Ramsgate with his sister. I do not believe at all that she is as sick as everyone thinks her to be. She wants to separate dear Mr. Bingley from us; I can feel it deep in my poor, sick heart. I do hope that she will not wish to live with you and Mr. Bingley after the wedding. At her age, she should look for her own husband. It is high time for her. I hope that she will not become a burden to Mr. Bingley when he has his own family."

"Caroline Bingley has a dowry of twenty thousand pounds," Elizabeth reminded her mother. "She will never be a burden to her family."

Mrs. Bennet was not convinced with such reasoning. "For now all her expenses are covered from Mr. Bingley's funds, though. It was all fine when he was a bachelor, but soon he will be a married man with responsibilities, and he should think of his wife and future children in the first place."

"Mama, I think that it is too soon to speak of such matters. Caroline is ill. We should concentrate on her regaining her health."

Mrs. Bingley sniffed. "I only hope that Mr. Bingley comes back to us soon."

Elizabeth began to read again while Jane and Mrs. Bennet returned to discussing the seating arrangement at the wedding breakfast. They were wondering where to sit Colonel Fitzwilliam, as he did not know anyone in the company apart from Darcy, Bingley and Georgiana.

The door opened, and Elizabeth did not even look up to see who entered, thinking that it was Mary coming from the music room, or Kitty and Georgiana, returning from the Lucas Lodge.

"Dear Mr. Darcy! You came at last!" Her mother's high-pitched voice drew her attention. On turning her head, she saw Darcy, standing stiff and awkward, as Mrs. Bennet hugged him around his midsection.

Elizabeth rose to her feet and made her way across the room hastily. "Mama, Mr. Darcy must be tired after the journey from London," she reminded gently.

"Oh, yes, naturally," the woman agreed, stepping back. "Are you hungry, Mr. Darcy? Would you like to eat something before dinner?"

"A cup of tea would be quite enough," Darcy said.

"I will see to it myself," Mrs. Bennet assured. "Jane, come with me, dear, I will need you."

Jane rose from her seat with a smile, then followed her mother.

Elizabeth and Darcy were left alone, looking at each other

for a moment longer, not saying a word.

Darcy spoke first. "Where is Georgiana?"

"She and Kitty are visiting Maria at Lucas Lodge."

Darcy nodded. "I see."

He was staring at her broodingly. Elizabeth reached for his hand, leading him to the sofa. As they sat down, she asked, "How is your business? Have you managed to deal with all the matters?"

"I have," he confirmed, closing her hand in both of his.

He was even less talkative than usual. Elizabeth refused to believe that he was still upset over her conversation with Colonel Fitzwilliam.

"You are pale, and look thinner," she noted, stroking his cheek with her free hand.

He leaned into her touch. "I had no appetite over the last week."

She smiled. "I am certain that my mother will be happy to change your mind in that respect."

He smiled back, but it did not reach his eyes.

"Fitzwilliam," she said, looking straight into his dark eyes, her hand still cupping the side of his face. "You cannot still be cross over my conversation with your cousin that evening in your townhouse."

Darcy leaned forward, putting his head over her shoulder. "I missed you," he confessed.

She stroked his hair. "I missed you too. I was wondering why you had not returned from London. Fitzwilliam, you cannot expect me to never again talk with Colonel Fitzwilliam. He has been a true friend to you and Georgiana over the years. We should treat him as such, both of us, you and I."

He turned his head slightly, kissing the side of her neck. "I simply want to be at Pemberley, you, Georgiana and I."

"I hear it quite often from you."

"It is the truth," he said, lifting his head to look into her eyes. "I am a very private man. This year has been especially disturbing, and it is due to you."

"Moi?" she asked innocently, pointing her finger at herself.

"Yes, you." He pulled her to him, her back to his front. "With the beginning of the year, I was trying to forget you. When I was convinced that I had been successful, we met again in Kent. Then I returned to Pemberley, hoping that in there I would erase your words from my memory. What you said to me that afternoon at Hunsford haunted me mercilessly."

Elizabeth shifted in his embrace while his arms closed around her tightly. "Colonel Fitzwilliam told me that he never again wishes to see you in the state that you were in when he visited Pemberley last May."

"He exaggerated. I was upset; however, there is no doubt that I deserved it."

Elizabeth turned her head to look at his face. "I think that he was warning me against hurting you again."

Darcy straightened up a little. "I am thankful for my cousin's good intentions. However, I am perfectly capable of protecting myself from harm and ensuring my own happiness. After all, I succeeded in winning your feelings and good opinion all by myself."

Elizabeth bit down on her lower lip. "May I remind you that Lady Catherine helped you to a certain point?"

"I prefer to believe that she only hurried the process. We would have met again because of Jane and Bingley's marriage even without my aunt's assistance. I would not have been able to stay away from you for a long time. And speaking of my relatives, my aunt and uncle agreed to come to our wedding."

Elizabeth sat up, pulling away from him. "The Earl and Countess of Matlock?"

"Yes, indeed. I was quite surprised myself when the letter arrived. Naturally, I informed them about our engagement. However, I never thought that they would even consider attending the wedding. They are still in good health, but they barely leave Matlock Hall these days."

"I am glad that they are coming," Elizabeth assured with caution in her voice. "However, I am afraid of their reaction towards Longbourn and my family."

"They made the decision to come, which in my opinion

indicates their acceptance of our union. Colonel Fitzwilliam must have been an excellent advocate for you."

"What about Lady Catherine? I am quite certain that she did everything in her power to present our situation in the least favourable light."

"Uncle did not mention Catherine in his letter, although I agree with you that she probably tried to convince them to her point of view. I know from Colonel Fitzwilliam that she even travelled to Matlock, even though she never travels north."

"Will they welcome me?" Elizabeth worried.

"Uncle wrote in his letter that I was my own man and he had no intention or right to interfere in my decisions. He also added that young, healthy, well-mannered and educated gentlemen's daughters, even though poor and without connections, might be a good choice, much better than some actress. He heard that you were from a family of many children; I believe that Lady Catherine referred to the Bennets as 'the brood' when she talked with him. Thus he hopes that we will have many children as well. Too few heirs have always been a great concern in our families."

"Why an actress?"

"He has a strong aversion to actresses since his eldest son's romance with one. Viscount Castlereagh, older brother of Colonel Fitzwilliam, wanted to marry one years ago. I was still a boy when it all happened, but I heard enough."

"Did your cousin marry her? The actress?"

Darcy chuckled. "Of course not. The Earl of Matlock would have never agreed to that. He married an heiress from Scotland, our distant cousin. Almost ten years after the wedding and they do not have a son, only one daughter. I think that uncle is afraid that the boy will not be born to them and there will be no one to carry on the family title. I think that he is determined to marry off Colonel Fitzwilliam, the sooner the better."

"I see. Is Colonel Fitzwilliam aware of those plans concerning his person?"

Darcy shrugged. "I believe so. He is quite devoted to his career, though."

Elizabeth sighed. "We should tell Mama that your uncle and aunt are coming. She will be beside herself with joy and worry."

"Why should she worry?"

"She has never admitted an earl and countess in her home. This will be quite an experience for her and for all of us as well."

Elizabeth looked down at their joined hands. Despite Darcy's reassurances, she was very much concerned over the Matlocks' reaction to her family. It was impossible to predict Mrs. Bennet's behaviour. She did not wish for Darcy to become alienated from his relatives, from his mother's brother, because of their marriage. It was enough that Lady Catherine would never accept their union.

"Look at me." Darcy touched her cheek, making her look into his eyes. "Do not fret over this. Uncle and Aunt will be gracious to you, your parents and sisters."

"I am more concerned over my mother's reaction to the news."

"The Matlocks wish to have good relations with me, thus they will do nothing to offend you. I am quite certain that Lord Matlock wishes for Colonel Fitzwilliam to marry Georgiana."

"But they are first cousins!" Elizabeth protested.

"Not exactly."

Elizabeth frowned, not understanding.

"Lord Matlock and my mother were half siblings because grandfather was married twice. My mother and Lady Catherine are the children from his second marriage."

"I see. Would you agree to such plans, of Colonel Fitzwilliam marrying Georgiana?"

"For now, I intend to give my uncle hope that I will not oppose it when the time comes. Trust me on that; the Matlocks will be kind and welcoming to you. I am certain that Colonel Fitzwilliam told them how much in love I was with you. They will not wish to alienate me now by disrespecting you."

"What about Georgiana?"

"What about her?"

"Does she know?"

"I doubt that she suspects anything of the kind. She is much too young to even think about marriage. I will worry about it in a few years. I do not plan to agree to any marriage for her until she is at least your age."

"Are you against Colonel Fitzwilliam?"

"As Georgiana's husband?"

She nodded.

"Not at all. I can trust him with her. She will be safe. They will live near Pemberley. I know that he will not hurt her. However, I do believe that there is time yet to consider it. Georgiana sees him as a brother. He is nearly fifteen years older than she."

"You are older than I am."

"Only seven years, not over a decade."

Their conversation was interrupted as Mrs. Bennet together with Jane and the maid entered, carrying a tray with tea and a cheesecake.

"Your favourite dessert, Mr. Darcy," Mrs. Bennet said, cutting out a generous helping of the cake and placing it on a small plate before passing it to Darcy.

Darcy murmured "thank you," then put the piece into his mouth, chewing slowly with a pleased expression on his face.

"Good?" Mrs. Bennet asked with a motherly smile, to which

Darcy nodded before swallowing and putting another piece into his mouth.

"I always have cheesecake, knowing how much you like it, Mr. Darcy. I will make sure that Lizzy passes the recipe to your cook at Pemberley."

Darcy stared imploringly at Elizabeth, not interrupting his eating. She understood that he wished for her to announce to Mrs. Bennet the arrival of his relatives.

"Mama, Mr. Darcy has some news to share," she said, gaining her mother's attention. Mrs. Bennet was sipping her tea, but thankfully she put the cup down in anticipation of hearing the news. Elizabeth did not wish for her to burn herself with hot liquid.

"What news?"

"There will be more guests attending the wedding."

"Oh?"

"Yes, Mr. Darcy's aunt and uncle will attend."

"They will?" Mrs. Bennet looked over at Darcy. "Where are they from? Have I heard about them before?"

"You have, Mama," Elizabeth answered. "You remember Mr. Collins mentioning them last year when he was visiting us? He told you about the brother of Lady Catherine de Bourgh."

Mrs. Bennet's blue eyes widened dramatically. "The Earl of Matlock?" she whispered.

At last Darcy decided to voice himself. "They will be arriving with the beginning of the next week, Monday probably."

"The Earl of Matlock," Mrs. Bennet repeated in awe.

Jane leaned over, touching her mother's arm. "Are you well, Mama?"

Mrs. Bennet turned her head to look at her eldest daughter. "In which room will we put them?"

"The guest room," Jane replied calmly.

Mrs. Bennet nodded. "The guest room."

"I am certain that Bingley would not mind if they stayed in Netherfield together with Colonel Fitzwilliam and I," Darcy proposed.

"Absolutely not!" Mrs. Bennet exclaimed in a high-pitched voice, making Darcy drop the piece of cheesecake on his black trousers. "Mr. Bennet will move to the guest room until the wedding. The Earl of Matlock and his wife will stay in his bedchamber."

"Mama, it is not necessary," Elizabeth protested, collecting up the pieces of fallen cake from Darcy's leg and the carpet.

"It is! Your father's room has fine furniture and it is much bigger than the guest room."

"What will Papa think of it?" Jane worried.

Mrs. Bennet made a dismissive wave of her hand. "He almost sleeps in the library, he will not mind moving to another room for a short time. I doubt that he will notice. Tomorrow we must go to Lady Lucas and later to my sister,

Mrs. Phillips. They have a few pieces that they should agree to lend to us."

"Mama!" Elizabeth cried out.

"Oh, shush. I am doing this for you. You do not wish for Mr. Darcy's family to think of us as beggars. Lady Lucas's crystal vases will look excellent in our drawing room, while Mrs. Phillips's blue Persian carpet will be placed in your father's bedroom, making it look less dreary."

Elizabeth felt her face growing hot, and she looked over at Darcy, nervous of his reaction to her mother's plans of borrowing finer pieces of furniture from the neighbours only to impress his relatives. But her fiancé was calmly drinking his tea.

"More cheesecake?" Elizabeth asked him weakly.

He nodded with a smile. "Yes, please."

As Elizabeth was cutting him another generous piece of his favourite dessert, she thought that there was probably nothing that could come from her family that would ever truly surprise him. He had indeed gone a long way in the last year.

CHAPTER THIRTEEN

Elizabeth ran down the hill, enjoying the feeling of freedom.

"Elizabeth!"

Still running, she looked up to see Darcy waving at her from behind the fence separating Longbourn's pasture from Netherfield. She waved, running faster. Soon she reached him, only slightly out of breath.

"Careful," he cautioned her, helping her to climb over the fence.

"I am quite adept at this," she boasted, hopping down straight into his arms.

"I am well aware of it," he said, smiling down at her, keeping her close to him. "Good morning," he murmured.

"Good morning," she whispered back.

They stared into each other's eyes for a long time. Elizabeth was certain that he would kiss her in a moment, but he did not. He only ran his hands down her back, asking, "Are you not cold?"

She shook her head. "No."

"Derbyshire is much colder than the south of England. I am worried that you will feel cold there."

"Mama ordered a new velvet coat with fur lining for me."

"That is excellent. However, Pemberley is a cold house. It is difficult to keep it warm in winter, especially the reception rooms. They are simply much too large to keep them properly heated. However, the family bedrooms on the second floor are usually warm and welcoming. Georgiana and I are used to lower temperatures in the house, but I am afraid that you may become sick."

"I shall be well, Fitzwilliam."

He kissed her forehead. "I will see to it." He took her hand in his and began walking.

"We are going to Netherfield?" Elizabeth asked.

"We are. I thought that we could have some privacy before Bingley's return. It is difficult to get a private moment at Longbourn these days."

"Are you sure that Mr. Bingley is truly returning?"

"He is."

"Tomorrow?"

"Yes, tomorrow. At least, from what I could decipher from his scribble."

Elizabeth sighed. "I am so relieved."

"Relieved? You thought that he would not come."

"I thought that Caroline would try to stop his marriage to Jane."

"You overestimate her. I hear that she is feeling better."

"Yes, she is. Mr. Bingley wrote about her improvement in his last letter to Jane. She will stay for a few months with Mrs. Hurst now that she is recovering. Mr. Bingley thinks that the company of a sister and a child will help to improve her mood."

"Let us hope so. For Bingley's sake."

"And Jane's," Darcy added.

"And Jane's," Elizabeth agreed.

Soon they reached Netherfield. Elizabeth was rather surprised when Darcy did not lead her to the drawing room or the library but directly upstairs and to his bedroom.

She walked into the spacious room with sparse furniture. Apart from the bed, there were only a few chairs and one small cabinet pushed against the wall. Jane for sure would be busy with finishing decorating the house. Many empty rooms gave the impression of an unlived house, especially upstairs.

Darcy closed the door, walking to her confidently, placing his hands on both sides of her waist. "Do you remember what I promised to you here at Netherfield the day before our departure to London?"

Elizabeth cocked her head to the side. "I do remember. You promised that you would try to find some private time for us."

"I believe that it is time to fulfil this promise."

"What about the restraint you talked about before?"

He ducked his head to kiss the side of her neck. "I had my reasons back then. Now that situation is quite different."

"Oh?"

"Our wedding is in exactly a week's time. Even if there are consequences to our actions, no one will notice or say anything," he murmured, nuzzling her neck. He pulled her to him, his hands running down her back, pressing her to him, cupping her bottom.

"Are you well?" he asked when she did not respond to his kisses and caresses with the ardour that he expected.

"Do you always plan everything?"

"No." He smiled down at her. "I certainly did not plan on meeting you."

She sighed, closing her eyes, hiding her face in his chest.

"You are unwell," he insisted.

"Forgive me, Fitzwilliam. I am exhausted. Mama is insufferable. Papa compared her today to a headless chicken running around the house."

Darcy chuckled. "Your father has a way with words."

"The house is unrecognisable. She moved around all the furniture, adding the pieces she borrowed from Lady Lucas and Mrs. Phillips. Do you know that she ordered new wallpaper for the drawing room?"

"She did?"

"The entire downstairs smells so badly now. You can develop a headache from only sitting there. I think that the walls cannot dry properly because it is so cold, even though there is always a fire in the mantelpiece. I do not think that this shade was a good choice; it is a very vivid green. It was Mama's intention, though, to brighten the room. She remembered how Lady Catherine had said during her visit that it was much too dark to serve as a drawing room."

"It is partially my fault. Perhaps I should have told her about my relatives' arrival a day before, or taken them directly to Netherfield and introduced them in the church."

"No, no, Mama would have been beside herself if she did not know that they were coming."

"Do not think about all this now," Darcy whispered, kissing her forehead. "Try to forget. In a few days we will be alone on our way to Derbyshire."

"Georgiana is coming with us," Elizabeth reminded.

"No, she is not. She will return with my aunt and uncle and Colonel Fitzwilliam. She will stay with them for a few weeks in Matlock."

"Will she not feel rejected? I do not wish her to think that her brother's wife wants to get rid of her as soon as possible."

"Nonsense," Darcy dismissed her worry. "This stay will be beneficial for her. The Matlocks are quite sociable. She should overcome her shyness and meet more people. I can already see a change in her after those few months spent in Hertfordshire."

"And she will have the opportunity to spend more time with

Colonel Fitzwilliam."

"Yes, indeed."

"Did he talk with you about his intentions towards Georgiana?"

"His intentions... I do not believe that he has any serious intentions as for now. Georgiana is still very young. He is willing to give both of them a chance to see whether there may be something more between them."

Elizabeth wished to ask more, but she decided to put the topic to rest. In her opinion, the age difference between Georgiana and Colonel Fitzwilliam was quite significant. Darcy, however, was rather sensitive when she discussed Colonel Fitzwilliam. He might take her further questions concerning Georgiana's possible marriage as another sign of personal interest in his cousin.

Darcy's hands moved to the front clasps of her pelisse, opening them slowly and pushing the thick material off her shoulders. He draped it over the nearest chair, before leading her to the bed. They sat on the edge of it and Darcy began kissing her in earnest, his hands roaming freely over her body.

Even though Elizabeth enjoyed his attentions, she could not relax. After a moment longer Darcy realized how unresponsive she was. He kissed her neck, murmuring, "Your mind is elsewhere."

"I am sorry."

He pulled back, cupping her cheek. "We do not have to do anything you do not feel ready for."

"I barely slept last night."

"You cannot fret over everything that is happening. You will become sick."

"There is one matter especially..."

"Yes?" Darcy waited patiently.

"Mama received a letter from Lydia."

Darcy frowned. "And?"

"Lydia does not understand why she and Wickham are not invited to our wedding."

"Is she that foolish, or simply pretending naivety, to even bother your mother with such enquiries?" Darcy asked harshly.

"Mama wrote to her a long time ago that they were not invited, I assure you."

"Good."

"However, Lydia does not seem to accept it."

Seeing her troubled expression, Darcy wrapped his arms around her. "Do not concern yourself with this, dearest. Wickham is not that stupid to come here."

"Lydia is unpredictable."

"She cannot travel on her own, not from Newcastle."

"I dreamed last night that she showed up at the church on our wedding day with Wickham behind her."

Darcy kissed her forehead, pressing her to him. "Perhaps she arrived together with Lady Catherine de Bourgh?" he chuckled against her hair.

"Do not jest!" she cried, pushing at his chest. "It is not amusing."

Darcy sighed, not letting her pull away from his arms. "You are tired and upset. You should rest." With those words he knelt in front of her, lifting her dress and petticoats to remove her boots. As her feet were freed from the sturdy boots, he put them neatly aside. Then he stood up and began removing his coat, vest, neck cloth and tall boots.

"Come," he said, extending his hand to her as he climbed onto the bed behind her.

"Fitzwilliam, I..." she began, hesitation in her voice, but he pulled her to him, her back to his front.

"You are in dire need of a nap," he announced.

Elizabeth snuggled deeper in his embrace as he draped a blanket over both of them.

"Sleep, my love," she heard before closing her eyes.

She felt safe and loved, peaceful for the first time in many days.

***

Elizabeth woke up hours later. Darcy was sleeping on his side, one of his legs draped over both of hers.

Sitting up, she yawned and looked around, searching for the clock to see the time. They should return to Longbourn. Not that their absence would be noticed in the commotion amidst the preparations.

"Fitzwilliam, wake up." She patted his chest. He murmured something before turning on his stomach, burying his head in a pillow.

Elizabeth slipped down from the bed, stretching herself. There was a clock on the mantelpiece and it read three o'clock.

She returned to the bed, shaking Darcy's shoulder. "Fitzwilliam, it is late. Wake up."

Finally he groaned and opened his eyes. Seeing her leaning over him, he smiled. "Come here." He tried to pull her back on the bed next to him.

She resisted joining him. "It is late. We should go."

He sat up. "What time is it?"

"Three o'clock."

He yawned into his fist, nodding his head. "You are right. I must return you to Longbourn. Your mother might think that I took you to Gretna Green."

Elizabeth sat down on the chair, putting on her boots. "I have begun to think that it would be quite a pleasant alternative."

"A few more days and it will be over. The next wedding celebration we will have to survive will be Georgiana's."

They dressed themselves and walked downstairs. They did not expect to see anyone apart from the butler or perhaps the housekeeper.

"Good day to you! I was about to wake you up."

"Bingley!" Darcy exclaimed. "I did not expect to see you today!"

"I could not stay a day longer away from my Jane. My first intention was to go directly to Longbourn, but as I was riding a horse from London I preferred to step by at Netherfield to wash up and change my clothes. You may imagine my surprise when the butler told me that you were in the house. I started looking for you, and only found you sleeping like babes in Darcy's room."

Darcy put his arm around Elizabeth. "We required some time alone."

Bingley laughed, looking at them with smiling eyes. "I can well imagine that!"

"My sister will be so pleased to see you," Elizabeth assured. "She missed you."

"As I missed her," Bingley replied.

"How is Miss Bingley?"

"Much better. She eats almost normally, and answers questions even though she does not speak as much as she used to. She seemed quite happy when I left her with Luisa and Hurst."

Darcy clasped his arm. "You are an uncle then."

Bingley nodded. "They have a healthy, fine boy. After so

many years without children it is indeed a happy event for them. I have not seen Hurst with a drink for the entire two days I spent with them."

"We are pleased that Miss Bingley is better," Elizabeth said graciously. Her feelings towards Caroline were much more favourable now when Mr. Bingley was back with them.

"Thank you, Miss Elizabeth. You are very kind indeed. Caroline would like to apologize to the both of you for her behaviour."

"It is not necessary," Darcy said, glancing at Elizabeth.

"She insisted."

"Does she intend to attend the wedding?" Elizabeth asked, fearing the answer.

"She is not well enough yet to come. We decided that she will stay with the Hursts, helping Luisa with the baby, keeping her company. Nevertheless, I am certain the she will apologize to both of you at the earliest opportunity."

Darcy and Elizabeth exchanged knowing looks. They did not anticipate the next meeting with Caroline Bingley, no matter how changed she was, according to her brother.

CHAPTER FOURTEEN

"Charles!" Jane exclaimed, running into the arms of her betrothed.

Bingley embraced Jane tightly, not minding the company of the Bennet family as well as Darcy and Georgiana among them.

As soon as Jane stepped back from her betrothed, Mrs. Bennet hurried to his side.

"Dear Mr. Bingley! It is so good to have you here with us. I was so concerned that you would abandon us. I have had bad dreams for the last several nights."

Bingley began to assure his future mother-in-law that he had no intention of ever leaving his dear Jane, which managed to calm Mrs. Bennet's nerves.

As Bingley was in the centre of everyone's attention, Elizabeth and Darcy managed to find a quiet corner for themselves by the window. Elizabeth stepped close to him, whispering, "I do not wish to see Caroline Bingley ever again."

"If she wishes to apologize, we cannot forbid her from doing so."

"Why?"

"Elizabeth, dearest, Caroline is Bingley's sister, this has not changed. We cannot pretend that she does not exist."

"You are ready to forget everything that she has done to Jane, to us," she accused.

"Charles thinks that she has learned from her past mistakes."

"You once told me that your good opinion, once lost, is lost forever."

"That has not changed. However, we should act civilly towards Caroline for Bingley's as well as your sister's sake."

Elizabeth crossed her arms over her chest. "I do not trust Caroline Bingley. I agree that she was ill that evening in London when she attacked us, but before that her actions towards Jane were cruel and calculated."

Darcy put his arm around her, bringing her close to him. "Caroline is not our concern, but Jane and Bingley's. We will not see her often."

"Poor Jane."

"Your sister is a clever and sensible woman. She will find a way to deal with Caroline."

Elizabeth looked into his kind and calm face. He knew how to calm her down when she became agitated.

"Mr. Darcy, Elizabeth, the tea is served!" Mrs. Bennet's voice carried through the air. "Come, come, we are not going to wait for you. You have had the entire day to speak privately."

Elizabeth blushed slightly at her mother's remark. Mrs.

Bennet had noticed Elizabeth's absence and rightly concluded that she had been in Darcy's company for the most of the day.

"Yes, Mama," Elizabeth answered, taking a seat next to Jane with Darcy sitting not far from her.

"Mama was worried about you when you disappeared in the morning," Jane whispered in her ear.

"I went for a walk."

"Not returning until four in the afternoon." There was a slight accusation in Jane's voice.

"We fell asleep at Netherfield."

Jane smiled. "I see."

"We truly fell asleep," she insisted, guessing her sister's line of thinking.

"Mama feared that you might have convinced Darcy into doing something foolish."

"Such as?"

"Gretna Green."

Elizabeth's eyes caught Jane's blue gaze for a moment longer. "Certainly not now, a few days before the wedding."

"Mama guessed right, then."

Elizabeth shook her head in denial. "Mama does not know Darcy as well as she thinks."

Jane sent her a questioning look but said nothing more. It seemed that Mr. Darcy could do nothing wrong in Mrs. Bennet's eyes.

***

"I was told that you had five daughters, Mrs. Bennet," Lady Matlock said, her eyes wandering around the room, stopping on Jane and Elizabeth, then Mary and Kitty.

Mrs. Bennet blinked before replying in a quiet, rather distinguished voice, "Yes, your ladyship. My youngest daughter was married this summer. She resides together with her husband in Newcastle."

"Quite a busy year for you it must have been, with three weddings in the family."

"We have been truly blessed, your ladyship. I cannot be more pleased for my daughters' happiness."

Elizabeth breathed out in quiet relief as she listened to the conversation. Her mother was calm and collected. She had not mentioned Wickham's name. Was it an accident or a conscious effort? Did Wickham not present himself as favourably as before now that he could be compared to much wealthier and more illustrious sons-in-law?

"You have a lovely home, Mrs. Bennet," Lady Matlock praised graciously. "Rather small, but I imagine quite comfortable and easy to upkeep."

"We enjoy it, although I would prefer for the park to be larger," Mrs. Bennet noted.

Reassured with her mother's performance, Elizabeth stepped closer to the other end of the room, where the Earl of Matlock sat in the company of Darcy and her father. From what she could overhear, it seemed that they were comparing the changes which Oxford university had undergone throughout the years, as Darcy finished it six years ago, Mr. Bennet thirty years ago and the Earl of Matlock forty years ago.

"Are you nervous, Miss Elizabeth?" she heard a male voice say. Turning around, she faced Colonel Fitzwilliam.

"Why should I be?" she enquired archly.

"Because you are marrying my cousin in merely four days' time."

"Not in the least."

"Oh? I heard that wedding nerves are a natural state that both man and woman find themselves in before their wedding day."

"To be entirely honest, Colonel Fitzwilliam, other matters overshadowed any nerves that I might have had. The concern over my family's performance on the wedding day as well as today when my father and mother are meeting your parents was constantly on my mind."

"I find your family very pleasant," he retorted. "Your father is a reasonable man, and your mother seems very much devoted to you and your sisters. It is all that she talks about. As for your sisters, they are very pleasant as well; the two youngest have taken to Georgiana."

They both looked across the room where Mary, Kitty and

Georgiana stood by the window, smiling and whispering some secrets to one another.

"When it comes to your elder sister, Miss Jane, she is stunningly beautiful. Much too handsome for Bingley."

"Mr. Bingley is a handsome man!"

"Still, you have to admit that he is not as attractive as your sister."

Elizabeth smiled proudly. "It would be very hard indeed to find another person, man or woman, who could match my sister's beauty."

"True, true. I still cannot understand why Darcy tried to convince Bingley that your sister was not suitable for him."

"As you may remember, Colonel Fitzwilliam, it was not my sister who was found lacking, but rather my family."

"Which I cannot understand, either."

Elizabeth looked into his light-coloured eyes. "You are very gracious, sir. I love my family, my mother, father and all my sisters. However, I am not blinded to their faults."

"Their faults are the same as the faults of any other family in England, I assure you."

"My family lacks connection and the standing in the world, though," she commented, "which makes their personal faults much more recognizable."

"I daresay that the position of the Bennet family has changed due to the excellent matches made by the two eldest daughters."

"Both Jane and I were fortunate enough to meet men whom we care for. My reasons for accepting your cousin were very selfish and personal. I thought about my happiness, not my family's fortune."

"Ah, yes. Darcy will never have a reason to think that you married him for his fortune."

"Only a year ago I was certain that I would never marry."

"A handsome, charming, intelligent and spirited woman like you?"

"I knew that I would not be able to marry someone for security. I would not be able to live with a person I did not love, share my everyday existence with him. Thus I thought that Jane would marry well, as she is so kind and beautiful, and I would live with her, helping her to raise her children."

Colonel Fitzwilliam watched her for a moment longer with a thoughtful expression written on his face. "Excuse me, Miss Elizabeth, but I find it rather difficult to believe."

"I am a realist, even a pessimist. I always envision the worst of what may happen, the dreariest scenario. I never thought that I would meet someone like Darcy, and as you know, at the beginning of our acquaintance I did not think very highly of him."

Their conversation was interrupted when Darcy walked over to them. "Tell me, Cousin," he spoke casually. "What is the reason that every time I see you, you seem to concentrate your entire attention on my lovely bride?"

Colonel Fitzwilliam smiled. "It is always a great pleasure to speak with Miss Elizabeth. You must have noticed that she is an interesting companion."

"Indeed she is," Darcy agreed, putting his arm around Elizabeth, pinning her closely to his side. "I cannot agree with you more, Cousin. I fully appreciate her company, I assure you. After all, most of her days and all her nights belong to me."

Elizabeth's mouth fell open as she stared at Darcy. She could barely believe her own ears.

Colonel Fitzwilliam seemed much less shocked with his cousin's retort. He smiled with good humour, bowed and walked away to talk with Bingley and Jane

"How could you?" Elizabeth whispered furiously.

"He heard what he deserved to hear."

"You provoked him in the first place. You could have simply asked what we discussed."

"You are defending him, then?"

"I am trying make your realize that you made a fool of yourself. Moreover, you humiliated me."

"I told him clearly and openly what I think about him paying too much attention to the woman who will become my wife within a few days."

Elizabeth took a calming breath, then spoke in a well-measured tone, "Fitzwilliam, Colonel Fitzwilliam is more like a brother to you than anyone else, you told me this yourself. He is your friend and mine as well, he supported us from the beginning."

"Let me remind you that it was partially of his doing that you rejected my first proposal."

"He had nothing to do with it," she protested.

"Truly? Nothing? He told you that it was I who convinced Bingley to abandon Jane the same day that I planned to propose."

"He never gave me any names. Even before, I had my suspicions when it came to your involvement with Jane and Bingley. Colonel Fitzwilliam only confirmed them."

"What a happy coincidence indeed! Right on the day of my proposal."

She stared at him in astonishment. "Fitzwilliam, you cannot possibly believe in what you are saying."

"I do believe that if he had my fortune, he would not hesitate even a moment to ask for your hand. I can see how he looks at you. He seeks your company. I will not tolerate that."

"You cannot forbid me from speaking to other people."

"But I can demand some respect from you. You should not be flirting with a single man who is enamoured of you right in front of both of our families and in my presence."

Elizabeth opened her mouth to answer such ridiculous

accusations, but perhaps for the first time when in Darcy's presence she lacked the right words.

***

"Can you believe it, Jane?" Elizabeth cried, pacing the room as Jane sat on the bed.

"Calm down, Lizzy."

"How can I be calm? Your Mr. Bingley does not forbid you from talking to other people."

"Perhaps you misunderstood Mr. Darcy."

"I understood him perfectly well. He said that he would not tolerate Colonel Fitzwilliam seeking my company and me flirting with him in front of both of our families. Those are his exact words, Jane."

"It must have sounded harsh to you, Sister, but I believe that Mr. Darcy said it when he was overwhelmed by strong emotions. Keep in mind that he is deeply in love with you and may feel jealous of another attractive man who has your attention."

"Colonel Fitzwilliam belongs to his family, and is more like a brother than a cousin to him. Darcy even mentioned to me about the possibility of a marriage between him and Georgiana in the future. He trusts him with his sister but he does not trust him to speak with me for longer than a short moment. It does not make any sense."

"Lizzy, put yourself in Mr. Darcy's situation. How would you react if you witnessed repeatedly that your beloved was having lengthy conversations with the one and same young, single and attractive woman? Would you not feel threatened?"

"It is not like that, Jane."

"Imagine if Mr. Darcy preferred mine or Kitty's company when you are in the room with him?"

"Jane, but—"

"Would you be pleased?"

Elizabeth thought for a moment. "No."

"There, you see? You have your answer."

"But Darcy—"

"Mr. Darcy has eyes only for you. He rarely addresses other women. He barely speaks even with me. Since your engagement I have seen him speaking for longer periods of time with Mama, Mrs. Gardiner, or his sister, and in most cases you were the sole subject of those conversations."

"Am I forbidden to speak to other men, then?"

Jane sighed. "Lizzy, I am trying to help you, but you are not listening. For your own good, I advise you to cut all your future interactions with Colonel Fitzwilliam short and sweet."

"For now I cannot even think about facing Colonel Fitzwilliam again. Oh, Jane, it was so mortifying and humiliating when Darcy said in front of Colonel Fitzwilliam that my days and nights belonged to him. I wanted to hide in the library and not leave before the morning."

"Mr. Darcy certainly made his opinion known."

Elizabeth dropped heavily on the bed, lying on her back. "He did."

"Lizzy, I think that you should be more concerned about facing Mr. Darcy, rather than his cousin."

"Insufferable man," Elizabeth murmured.

"Who?" Jane asked innocently.

Elizabeth shot her an exasperated look. "Darcy, naturally!"

"His character should not be of much surprise to you by now."

"Jane, you are not helping me!"

"Forgive me, Lizzy," Jane apologized quietly. "It was not my intention to upset you even more."

The sisters were silent for a moment longer. At last Elizabeth said, sitting up, "You are correct, though, that my next conversation with Fitzwilliam Darcy will not be an easy one."

CHAPTER FIFTEEN

"What a year it has been," Jane marvelled. "This time last year I was in despair over Mr. Bingley's departure, fearing that I would never see him again."

Elizabeth smiled. "And tomorrow you will marry him."

The sisters were sitting on Elizabeth's bed, in her mostly empty bedroom. The room would soon be redecorated for Kitty.

"And you and Mr. Darcy!" Jane exclaimed softly. "Who would have thought?"

Elizabeth laughed. "Certainly not I."

Jane watched her sister closely. "Did you have the opportunity to talk with Mr. Darcy?"

Elizabeth's expression fell. "There was no time for that. I tried to find a private moment. However, Darcy was less eager to do so."

"Is he avoiding you?"

"On the contrary. He seeks my company as always, but we have been constantly surrounded by people these days."

"It is not my desire to pry, Lizzy, but it does not seem a particularly sound idea to say the marriage vows when you two are in disagreement."

Elizabeth sighed. "I am aware of it, Jane. Darcy behaves as if nothing has happened between us."

"You feel differently, though."

"I will talk to him," Elizabeth promised with determination.

"Tomorrow, before the wedding?" Jane guessed.

"Rather after the ceremony on our way to Derbyshire. It will be the first opportunity to speak with him privately in days."

"Derbyshire!" Jane exclaimed softly. "It is so far away."

"It is. I cannot believe that we will not able to see each other every other day."

"I had never even considered such a possibility that one day we would live in different parts of the country."

"It does not have to be like that."

Jane gave her a questioning look. "You told me yourself that Mr. Darcy prefers the country and cannot imagine spending an entire year in London away from Pemberley."

"Your Mr. Bingley, however, has not yet decided whether he wants to make Netherfield his permanent residence," Elizabeth pointed out quickly.

"He has not," Jane confirmed.

"Convince him to consider moving to the north. It does not have to be in Derbyshire; the neighbouring county would do."

Jane hesitated. "Charles never mentioned the possibility of living in the north."

Elizabeth wrapped her fingers around her sister's wrists,

looking into her blue eyes. "Jane, Darcy will never leave Pemberley, nor will he ever want to live in London, but Mr. Bingley is free to choose where he will buy his estate. Convincing him to move north is our only chance for us to see each other more than twice a year."

The knock at the door interrupted their conversation. Mrs. Bennet entered, dressed in her nightclothes, her hair twisted in curling papers. "There you are! I have been looking for you, Jane, but it is good that I can talk to Lizzy as well."

Mrs. Bennet settled on the chair, facing her two eldest daughters, placing her hands neatly on her lap. "Jane, Elizabeth, tomorrow you will leave this house and begin a new life. You both are marrying good, wealthy men, and I am proud of you."

Elizabeth and Jane exchanged surprised looks. They were not expecting a speech like this from their mother on the eve of their wedding.

Their mother continued, "I am your mother, so it is my duty to give you my advice and guide you. Tomorrow evening, you will...you will..."

"Mama, we are aware what will happen tomorrow night," Jane said quickly, guessing the woman's intention.

"We have been raised in the country, after all," Elizabeth added.

Mrs. Bennet nodded, looking relieved. "I am pleased that

there is no need to explain the mechanics to you. There are still matters you should know of. Firstly, the first time with your husband will be painful, or at the very least uncomfortable. You have to bear it. Thankfully, it will not last long. My advice is to close your eyes, spread your legs, clench your teeth and think of England. It is not my wish to frighten you. You may expect that with time, a little practise and familiarity, you will learn to enjoy the marriage bed. Especially since both Mr. Darcy and Mr. Bingley are young, strong and handsome, as well as even-tempered and caring towards you. However, if you find yourself not particularly inclined to the act, there are ways to avoid it, such as headaches or citing tiredness. However, I am not advising you to do it until after you give birth to at least one or two children, boys preferably, when your position is secured. Do you understand?"

"Yes, Mama," the sisters answered in unison.

"Do you have any questions?"

"No, Mama."

"Good, good, excellent." Mrs. Bennet stood up. "I will bid you good night. Do not stay too late, otherwise you will look a fright tomorrow with dark circles under the eyes."

As the sisters were left alone, Elizabeth spoke first, "I did not expect that Mama would want to discuss this with us."

"She was very embarrassed," Jane noted.

"She was relieved that we did not ask any questions."

"I do not blame her. It must be difficult to speak of such intimate matters with one's daughters." Jane moved to the edge of the bed. "I should go, Lizzy. Mama is right, we should retire early."

"I will not be able to fall asleep."

Jane found her slippers and leaned over to hug her sister. "Good night, Lizzy."

"Good night," Elizabeth responded. "Please, promise me that you will think about what we spoke of before Mama came."

"I will, Sister."

Elizabeth put down the candle and lay down on her back. She closed her eyes, but she did not have the slightest urge to sleep. How could she? She knew that Jane was right, that she should have discussed the matter of Colonel Fitzwilliam with Darcy. However, it was also the truth that she and Darcy had barely had a moment to themselves for the last days. Darcy did not seem upset with her, though, treating her with his usual consideration, tenderness and kindness. Colonel Fitzwilliam, on the other hand, barely acknowledged her, staying on the other side of the room from her.

She turned on her side. Tomorrow she would be a married woman. It would be long months before she saw her family. She would have a new family, though, her new place in the world. How could she fall asleep? So many changes were coming with her new life having its start tomorrow.

***

Elizabeth waved dutifully at the slowly disappearing crowd of family, friends and neighbours gathered in front of her childhood home.

As soon as they were on the road leading to Meryton, Darcy, who was seated in front of her, reached to close the window. "It is a cold day. I do not wish for you to become sick on the journey."

Those were the first words he had spoken directly to her today. The wedding ceremony and the wedding breakfast had been a blur of many faces, smiles, cheers and good wishes.

"I am quite warm," she assured him. She felt almost too warm, dressed in her thick, new, dark-purple velvet coat lined with fur.

"Finally," Darcy breathed in relief. He removed his top hat and gloves. "No more parties, dinners, gatherings, or people constantly surrounding us, only you and I." He stretched his long legs in front of him and closed his eyes, his body relaxing visibly.

He seemed to enjoy the silence, thus Elizabeth decided not to interrupt the peacefulness he craved so much. She occupied herself with gazing out of the window at the familiar passing scenery. As they were driving through the high street of Meryton, she looked at the familiar shops which she often visited with her sisters. When would be the next opportunity to go on a stroll with her sisters? A year? Perhaps even longer.

"You looked beautiful today, Mrs. Darcy," Darcy's voice rumbled at her ear.

Turning her head, she looked into his face. He leaned for a kiss, his fingers working on the bow at her chin, untying it, pushing back her bonnet.

"Fitzwilliam, we should—" she started, but her words turned into a gasp when his hand slipped inside her coat, cupping her breast through the fine lace of her wedding dress.

Fighting the temptation of surrendering completely to the pleasure brought by his touch, she spoke clearly, "We should discuss the matter of Colonel Fitzwilliam."

Darcy's movements stopped, and he went completely still. "I do not see the point in discussing my cousin." His hand on her chest busied itself again, his fingers opening the side clasp of her dress.

Trying her best to ignore his hand now stroking gently her bare flesh, she said, "We must speak about what happened that evening and about what you said to me."

Darcy sighed, kissing her cheek. Without removing his hand from her bosom, he shifted her so that her back was to his chest. With his arms around her, he pulled her to him in a tight and secure embrace.

"You cannot forbid me from speaking with other people,

men or women," she said, settling against him.

"I did no such a thing."

"You accused me of flirting with him, which was not the case."

"Was it not?"

"Since our engagement, every conversation I had with Colonel Fitzwilliam has been related to you or to our wedding plans."

"For my peace of mind, I would ask you to restrain yourself from discussing me or our marriage with him." His voice was quiet and gentle but with a note of seriousness to it.

"I do understand your point, I truly do," she spoke fervently. "I would not be pleased if I saw you speak with an eligible and attractive young lady for longer that the exchange of simple greetings or pleasantries."

"There, you see, I was correct," he said, clearly pleased with her admission, resting his chin on her shoulder.

"However, you should not have said to your cousin that my nights belonged to you."

"It is the truth," he stated. "Or at least it will be from this night on," he added in a low voice.

"Fitzwilliam," she groaned, losing her patience. "It was entirely unnecessary."

"I do not regret saying it," he insisted. "I will not apologize if you expect this from me."

"Can you imagine how I felt? How humiliating it was to me?"

"Forgive me, then, if I caused you discomfort," he spoke stiffly. "It was not my intention. Nevertheless, you can be well assured now that such a situation will not be repeated in the future. My cousin understood my meaning very well."

"I will not be able to look him in the eye the next time we meet," she complained. "I cannot avoid talking to him forever, as I have done for the last couple of days."

"That is good."

Elizabeth turned into his embrace, pushing at his chest. "You do not feel in the least ashamed of what you have done," she accused.

"I do not," he agreed merrily. "If you cannot imagine yourself looking him in the eye, it means that you will not engage him in lengthy conversations as was your custom."

"What about your friendship with Colonel Fitzwilliam? Will you allow it to suffer because of your unnecessary remarks?"

"Our friendship is as good as ever," Darcy claimed. "Richard goaded me that evening, and not for the first time. We know each other very well, Elizabeth, and I can assure you that he does not hold ill feelings towards me. If anything, he is amused with the entire situation."

"I am not amused," Elizabeth deadpanned.

Darcy pulled her to him, placing her head on his chest, to

which she did not protest. "Can we put this topic to rest?" he asked.

"You refuse to see any reason, thus I do not see the point of continuing," she murmured.

"Good." He kissed her forehead and nose. "You are cold."

"A little," she admitted, snuggling deeper into his embrace.

"This is why I try to avoid travelling in winter for longer distances," he said.

Elizabeth was confused when he pushed her gently away from him and began removing something from under the seat.

"Come here." He motioned for her to cling to him again before covering both of them with lush, dark fur. "Better?" he asked after a moment, rubbing her back.

She nodded sleepily, yawning into the fine cloth of his great coat.

"Tired?" he whispered, his fingertips stroking the side of her face.

She nodded again, this time closing her eyes.

"Sleep," he ordered softly, his arms tightening around her with such strength that it was for a moment painful.

"I love you, my dearest Elizabeth," she heard before slipping into obliviousness.

CHAPTER SIXTEEN

Elizabeth entered the spacious chamber with small square windows. Darcy was right behind her.

"Is it to your satisfaction?"

She looked over her shoulder, smiling at him reassuringly. "Very much so."

They walked to the door, opened it and stepped into the smaller bedchamber. Elizabeth noticed that one of the trunks, the one with all her travel necessities, already stood by the window.

"Are you certain that you will manage without a maid tonight?"

"I have managed for one and twenty years, I do believe that I shall be fine for a few more days."

"Mrs. Reynolds assured me in her letters that she had selected your lady's maid very carefully and that you would be pleased with her."

"I am certain that I will be," Elizabeth agreed.

"If not, you can always pick someone else."

She smiled again. "I know."

He took one step closer. "Well then..." he cleared his throat.

She gave him a questioning gaze.

Leaning down, he kissed her cheek, his lips lingering on the corner of her mouth. "I shall see to our people, and later we should have dinner in here, unless you wish to go downstairs to the common area."

"Oh, no. I have seen too many people in the recent days. I crave privacy."

"Very well then. I will ask to send dinner in...." he hesitated, looking at her questioningly, "half an hour?"

"Yes. Excellent."

He bowed his curly head before leaving the room.

Elizabeth sat on the edge of the bed, looking around the small space. The bed seemed sturdy and inviting, the linens freshly laundered and ironed.

Half an hour. She had a little time to refresh before his return. She had to prepare herself for the night.

Kneeling in front of her trunk, she opened it. Right at the top there was a nightgown with matching robe, and slippers. Jane had received identical nightclothes.

She disrobed herself quickly, trembling against the slight chill in the room. She had some trouble with removing her stays. It was not only new, but also fastened tighter than she was used to.

Only in her stockings and shift, she walked to the nightstand and washed herself the best she could. She had taken a bath yesterday evening, washing her hair, and she still felt clean. She unpinned her hair, brushed it and plaited it into a loose braid.

She was hanging her clothes properly on a hood behind the screen so they would not become crumpled over the night when there was a knock on the door.

"Yes?"

"The dinner is here, Elizabeth."

She was surprised how fast half an hour had passed. "I am almost ready."

Hastily she put on her nightgown, robe and slippers.

When she stepped out, Darcy was standing by the table behind one of the chairs, his fingers gripping the green upholstery. His dark eyes settled on her form for a long time. He was not wearing his great coat anymore, but apart from that he was fully attired, including his neck cloth and long boots. Suddenly she felt underdressed. He did not seem disapproving of her informal outfit—on the contrary.

Elizabeth smiled as she made her way to the middle of the room, taking a seat on a chair he guarded.

His warm hands rested on her shoulders, giving them a gentle squeeze. "You look lovely," he said, bending down to kiss her temple.

He sat on a chair in front of her. They ate in silence. Elizabeth enjoyed the warm soup and some cold meat, while Darcy seemed more preoccupied with staring at her rather than consuming his own meal.

"Are you tired?" he asked.

"Not particularly," she answered. "I slept in the carriage," she reminded him.

He nodded but said nothing.

"Thank you," Elizabeth said, putting her napkin away, signalling that she had finished. "It was delicious."

"It is still quite early," Darcy noted. "Not even eight. We may read or sit by the fireplace before we retire for the night."

"How early in the morning do you plan to start our journey?"

"Seven."

"Then we should retire without delay. It was an eventful day, and we both need rest."

"Very well," he agreed, his expression eager. "I will call the servants to clean after dinner and then I will join you," he said, looking straight into her eyes.

"I would like to take a bath tomorrow morning."

He nodded. "I will see to it."

Elizabeth returned to the bedroom. She could hear Darcy's voice through the door as he talked to the servants. In order to occupy herself with some meaningful task, she found her brush. Usually it was Jane who brushed her hair every evening, but this task would now belong to her new maid. She was curious about who Mrs. Reynolds had selected, hoping that she would like and trust her.

The door opened without a knock and Darcy stepped in. "Your bath will be ready at six, the breakfast half an hour later."

"Excellent, thank you," Elizabeth said, putting her brush away and pleating her hair anew.

"Leave it."

Turning her head, she looked up at him. He was in the process of removing his vest, his coat already hanging neatly over the back of one of the chairs.

"Your hair. Let it free."

"It will tangle."

"Please."

Elizabeth considered his request. She knew that her hair would be difficult to deal with in the morning if she left it free for the night, but she decided to grant his wish. It was a small thing to make him happy. Allowing her long hair to rest against her shoulders and back, she stepped to the bed. She removed her robe and slippers before quickly climbing under the covers before Darcy could catch a glimpse of her form. While the robe was modest enough, the nightgown itself was indecent. It had long sleeves and high neckline but it was completely see-through. It was a farewell present from Mrs. Gardiner when Jane and Elizabeth had been leaving London.

Elizabeth heard Darcy walking around the room, removing his boots and lastly washing himself. She lay down with her back to him, wishing to give him privacy while he was finishing his toilette.

The bed dipped on the other side and Elizabeth pulled the sheet even higher up to her neck.

"Are you cold?" His deep voice rumbled above her ear as his arm draped over her. "There is no fireplace in this room. I will ask for hot bricks to be brought."

Elizabeth shifted on her back, looking into his concerned face. "I am not cold."

He studied her face for a long moment. "My dearest," he spoke tenderly. "You must know that we do not have to do anything you do not feel ready for tonight. I know that you are tired, as the last weeks have been exhausting for you."

She stroked his cheek. Here was truly the best of men, and he belonged to her. "You are very kind."

"We have time, a great deal of time, our entire lives. No matter what your mother told you about the marriage bed, I do not wish for you to be scared of me."

"My mother?"

"I imagine that she gave you some of her wisdom concerning marriage."

Elizabeth smiled. "She did. However, she did not scare me."

His expression told her that he did not quite believe her. "That is good, then."

"I am nervous about my nightgown," she blurted after

another moment of prolonged silence.

"Nightgown?" He frowned, thinking for a moment. "You do not wish to remove it?" he guessed.

"I do not wish for you to see it."

"I see. I will put the candles down."

Darcy took his time, walking around the bed to extinguish all the candles until the room was pitch-dark. He must see like a cat, because he found his way to the bed without any trouble.

He lay down on his side, close to her, his thigh pressing against her hip. "We may wait until we are at Pemberley," he whispered.

"I do not wish to wait," she said, the words easier to say in the dark. "I want you."

It was all the encouragement he needed. Their lips met. Those kisses were different than what she was used to. They were urgent and insistent. He wasted no time to reach to the neckline of her gown, tugging at the ribbons at the opening. Soon his hand slipped under the thin material to cup her breast. Elizabeth wrapped her arms around him, wishing him to know that she welcomed his attentions.

"I love you," he murmured into her neck, his voice elated.

"I love you too," she whispered back.

His hand moved down her body, reaching for the hem of her nightgown, which was tangled around her knees. He pulled the material up to her waist, his hand curling around the side of her hip.

"Will you sit up?" he asked, and when she did, he finished removing her gown, tossing it away. His own nightshirt followed seconds later.

Elizabeth gasped as he knelt between her legs and slowly lowered himself onto her body. Her heart began to race wildly as she felt him skin to skin.

His fingers combed through her hair and he murmured, "My dearest, loveliest Elizabeth."

His hand moved down her body, stopping for a moment on her breast, then his fingers circled her belly button before settling between her legs. At his first touch she stiffened, but after a few minutes of light stroking she relaxed enough to enjoy his caresses.

The darkness of the room enveloped her like warm, thick mist, making her regret that she had asked to put down the candles. She could hear her own laboured breathing and her moans, which to her ears resembled cries, as her husband left a trail of delicate kisses down her body, on her chest, waist, top of her thighs.

"My love," he whispered, his hand finding her face, cupping her cheek.

"Fitzwilliam," she breathed, pulling his head down for a kiss, which he enthusiastically returned.

"May I?" he asked, nudging her legs farther apart, settling

heavily between them.

"Yes."

"It will hurt the first time."

In response she ran her hand down his back to the narrowing of his waist, pressing down, telling him that she was ready.

The pain was the first thing she felt, stinging and deep, as if something sharp cut into her body. She pressed her lips tight, not to make a sound, not to worry him.

"Are you well?" he asked, his trembling hand touching her face.

"It is rather uncomfortable," she lied.

He sighed audibly. "It will pass. Allow me..." He cupped her knee, draping her leg around his side, surging deeper into her. Elizabeth saw bright stars dancing in front of her eyes, but they were not the result of pleasure, but a new wave of surging discomfort. Her mother had been right saying that it would hurt. She prayed that this torture would end soon.

He began to move at last, panting and moaning above her. For the first time this night she did not feel the connection with him despite the fact that they were intimately joined. She turned her face to the side, noticing that the worst pain was gone. Still, the feeling of unnatural fullness was far from enjoyable. She breathed out in relief when seconds later Darcy groaned deeply, trembling above her. Then he dropped lifelessly down next to her, his head on her shoulder, his hand stretched out, cupping her breast.

Within minutes his breathing calmed, and she thought that he'd fallen asleep, but then he moved.

"Can I light the candle now?" he asked.

"Yes," she replied, reaching down for the sheet to cover herself. Smoothing her hair, she sat up against the headboard.

Darcy moved to the other side of the bed, lighting the two candles on the bedside table.

Elizabeth blinked her eyes at the dim light filling the small room.

Her husband was beside her within seconds, cradling her to him. "Forgive me, dearest," he whispered fervently, kissing her cheek and lips. "I know that I hurt you."

Elizabeth's heart melted at his kindness. "I am well, Fitzwilliam. It could not be avoided."

"I love you," he assured.

"As I love you," she smiled up at him.

Her assurances calmed him down, and he lay back on his back, guiding her to rest on his chest. He was silent, kissing her head from time to time, his fingers tracing patterns on her bare arms and back.

Elizabeth felt sleepy, but the dull ache between her legs was difficult to ignore. She felt that once cleaned she would feel much better.

"Will you turn around for a moment please?" she asked, propping herself up on her elbow to look into his face. "I would like to clean myself," she explained hastily, seeing confusion written on his face.

"Of course."

Elizabeth pulled one of the sheets from the tangled mess of the bedcovers and wrapped it around herself.

She moved to the edge of the bed and planted her feet on the hardwood floor. Her legs felt boneless, and she had to put an effort into walking straight. She stepped to the washstand, reaching for a clean cloth, turning her head to make sure that Darcy was not looking at her. He kept his word as usual, facing the other side of the room.

She cleaned herself quickly, wincing slightly at the cool, wet cloth touching her tender flesh. When she was done she returned to bed.

Darcy gathered her to him, kissing her lightly on the lips. "Are you well?" he enquired, searching her eyes.

She smiled encouragingly. "Very well indeed." It was the truth. The slight throbbing was still present, but she felt much better after washing herself. The love in Darcy's eyes when he looked at her made her forget any discomfort.

He must have understood her words quite differently than she meant them, though, as he began to kiss her in earnest again, his hand running down and up her sheet-clad body.

"Do you think that we could...?" he whispered in her ear.

"Again?"

He smiled sheepishly. "There is no rule that only one time a night is allowed."

CHAPTER SEVENTEEN

Elizabeth returned his smile. She was not particularly eager to repeat the experience so soon. Nevertheless, she guessed that the act would happen many times in the coming weeks and months. Also, she reminded herself of her mother's assurances that only the first time would be painful.

She ran her hand down his back, admiring how broad and strong his shoulders were.

"Can we leave the candles?" he asked, kissing a path along her collarbone. "I want to see you."

Not waiting for her answer, he propped himself up on his lean but muscular arm, hooking his finger behind the sheet which was still wrapped around her, pulling it decidedly down. Elizabeth looked away. Such intimacy was still very new to her. Perhaps she should have asked for a glass of wine at dinner; it would surely have made her feel less inhibited.

She shuddered and moaned when he kissed the underside of her breast.

"Look at me," Darcy pleaded, cupping her cheek.

Elizabeth opened her eyes. His loving expression took her breath away for a moment. She had never felt so beloved by him.

The second time was easier; the feeling of having her husband inside of her was alien, but also exciting, and mostly pain free.

They snuggled together under the covers with Elizabeth's face in the crook of his neck.

"I am tired," Darcy revealed as his fingers stroked her back.

Elizabeth nuzzled the skin of his throat with her nose. The shadow of his day-old stubble tickled her, making her wrinkle her nose. "Let us sleep," she proposed, yawning.

"I do not wish to fall asleep. You are mine at last. We are together."

Lifting her head, she looked into his eyes. "We have been together for the last three months. I have been yours for all this time."

He shifted her in his embrace so she was now on her back and he hovered over her. "You are Mrs. Darcy now. There is quite a difference, I would say."

She smiled. "I suppose that there is."

He leaned down for a kiss. "Mrs. Darcy," he murmured.

Elizabeth responded to the kiss, but she was quite concerned that he would wish to engage in intimacy one more time. Who would have expected that? Especially with the reticence he displayed during their engagement. She did not wish to refuse him, but at the same time she was exhausted and aching in more places than one.

"Fitzwilliam," she spoke quietly as he was concentrated on kissing her neck, his hand curling around her hip.

"Yes, my love?"

Elizabeth cupped his face to look into his eyes. What she saw in them stopped her from saying anything. So much love and longing—how could she refuse him if he wished for it?

"My Lizzy," he murmured, carefully joining their bodies again.

The last clear memory of her wedding night was her husband falling into her embrace, his hot, laboured breath on her shoulder. She must have fallen asleep then too, and quite soundly. She woke up close to dawn to tend to her necessities with her husband wrapped tightly around her.

***

"Lizzy, wake up. Lizzy." She heard Darcy's voice, his gentle hand shaking her arm, but she refused to open her eyes. She felt as if she had fallen asleep only an hour ago, which was close to the truth. When she had gotten up around five, she was quite successful in waking her husband as well. If it had not been mortifying enough to use a chamber pot while being in the same room with him, even though separated by the screen, she had to listen to him doing exactly the same soon after. Then he thought that it was a good idea to engage her in another session of lovemaking. This time he had laid down on her from behind, lifting her bottom up by putting a pillow underneath it. Elizabeth had been much too stunned to protest. How could she face him now when they were not shrouded by convenient semidarkness? Four times in one night! Surely it was not expected behaviour!

She felt cold air hitting her as he removed the sheet from her.

"Your bath will turn cold," he threatened.

At last she opened her eyes. The curtains around the bed were closed, but the daylight was peeking through them.

"What time is it?" she croaked.

"Eight."

"Eight? We were supposed to depart at seven!"

"There is no hurry," he assured. "You slept so soundly. I know that you did not have a peaceful night."

Elizabeth ignored his smug expression. She winced upon sitting up. Her back hurt, her bottom as well, and her head pounded. She wondered whether there was a part of her that was not tender.

"Come," Darcy said, opening the bed curtains.

It was a sunny day, and Elizabeth squinted her eyes against the sudden light. She tried to cover herself with her hands, and on seeing her embarrassment, Darcy reached for her robe, helping her into it.

Elizabeth thanked him with gratefulness. He must think that she was silly to shy away from him after last night, when not only had he seen but also touched every part of her, but in the bright daylight her inhibitions returned.

There was a small bathtub near the door. She must have slept through the servants bringing it in and filling it with water.

On shaky legs she walked across the room, and with the help of her husband she climbed into the tub.

She moaned quietly as she submerged into very warm—almost hot—water. Bringing her legs to her chest, she supported her cheek on her knees and closed her eyes. She wanted to return to bed.

"Do you wish me to wash your hair?" Darcy asked.

Elizabeth had not planned to wash her hair today, but after last night she probably needed a good scrub all over, considering how sweaty she felt on falling asleep.

"Yes, thank you," she agreed, yawning widely into her open palm. She enjoyed his gentle ministration to her hair and was disappointed when he finished, wrapping a large towel around her head. Next he washed her back.

"Will you manage with the rest?" he asked, placing a soft cloth and a bar of soap in her hand.

She nodded. "I will."

He leaned down to kiss her forehead. "I will see you soon at breakfast. Call me if you need anything."

She smiled at him, wishing to convince him that she was

well. He smiled back, and after another kiss, this time to her nose, he departed. Only when he was walking away from her did she notice that he was already dressed, including his long boots and cravat. Only the sleeves of his shirt were rolled up to above his elbows. His step was energetic, his silhouette straighter and taller than usual. She could barely move, and he was strutting like a soldier on a parade.

Elizabeth was left alone. Still very much sleepy, she began cleaning herself, rubbing her skin gently with a soaped cloth. Her skin felt overly sensitive, and some places, like her neck, breasts and inner thighs, were so tender that it was painful to touch them.

She sat in the tub for the longest time, until the water turned cold. She could not find the strength to finish her bath. She knew that she had to move soon. Darcy had already knocked at the door enquiring if she was well.

Groaning in a most unladylike fashion, she climbed out of the tub, wrapping herself in a large towel left for her. She felt as if she was eighty and not one and twenty.

To her surprise, she discovered that earlier Darcy had hung out one of the new long-sleeved dresses made of thick but soft wool, perfect for a day of journey in winter. He acted as her lady's maid. A man of many talents he was.

Finally she managed to dress herself successfully, leaving her still-damp hair free, hanging down her back so it could dry.

Watching her reflection in the mirror, she smoothed down the wayward curls forming at her ears and forehead. She looked the same as yesterday, the only difference was that her cheeks were unnaturally flushed as if she had fever, and her lips were visibly swollen, the same as her eyes.

"I was worried," Darcy greeted her, waiting for her on the other side of the door.

"I am sorry. It took me longer than usual."

He put his arm around her, leading her to the table. "Come, they brought fresh tea only a minute ago."

He prepared her tea the way she liked. Elizabeth tried not to wince when she sat down. Her mother did not mention severe backache as the result of marital relations. Her husband moved with his usual grace, and contrary to her, he did not seem to be ailing from any kind of physical discomfort. Must be all those years of horse riding that gave him the advantage she did not have.

Elizabeth drank her tea, enjoying the fragrant liquid warming her insides.

"I examined your nightgown while you were sleeping," Darcy mentioned.

She gaped at him silently.

"I was curious why you did not wish me to see it last night."

"It is indecent."

"It is," he agreed happily, grinning at her widely, showing all his teeth. "A present from your mother?"

"No, Aunt Madeline."

"I will have to thank Mrs. Gardiner at the very first occasion," he spoke seriously, with a straight face. "But first I will insist on seeing you in it."

Elizabeth rolled her eyes, deciding to ignore his remark about thanking her aunt for gifting her a completely see-through item of clothing. They both knew that he would never do such a thing.

"It would be as good as seeing me without it," she retorted.

"I disagree." He reached to touch her hand, his thumb stroking her knuckles. "It would be most enticing."

"Perhaps you should wear it instead of me, then," she challenged, taking a bit of bread smeared with butter.

He laughed out loud. He was in a terribly good mood this morning. There was no doubt of that.

***

After breakfast, Darcy made sure that Elizabeth's hair dried completely. She sat with her back to the buzzing fireplace as he read the fresh newspaper, holding her hand the entire time. It was nearly midday when they finally began their journey anew. Elizabeth feared that in such a pace they would reach Pemberley in a week's time and not within three days as it was planned.

The weather was sunny, and Elizabeth tried to enjoy the

passing countryside, but her back ached so that it was difficult to even lean over to look out of the window.

Darcy's arm wrapped around her. "Come here," he said, bringing her to him.

Gratefully she snuggled against him.

"Are you well?" he enquired.

"My back hurts," she acknowledged at last. It was not her intention to worry him, but she was becoming too miserable to care.

He chuckled. "I noticed you walked funny."

With all her might, she pushed away from him. "Funny? Am I funny to you?" she demanded. "It is all your fault!" she accused.

He tried to bring her back into his arms, but she struggled. "My love, you are simply not familiar with such a form of physical exertion," he rationalized. "Your muscles are sore, but it is only natural. With time and practise you will become accustomed to it."

"You do not seem to be ailing from any discomfort." She eyed him warily through narrowed eyes.

"I am sorry that you are unwell, I truly am. Now, come to me, let me ease your pain."

Elizabeth leaned back into his embrace. He put his arm around her, bringing her to his chest. With his other hand he began to press his digits to her sore lower back, making her moan in relief as the tension slowly disappeared from her strained muscles.

Before long she fell asleep with one thought on her mind: How would she survive another night like the last one? She doubted if tomorrow morning she would be able to move from the bed on her own.

CHAPTER EIGHTEEN

Elizabeth looked out of the window at the passing countryside, not being able to take her eyes away from it for even the shortest moment. Everything was white, from the smallest twigs to the vast expanses of the fields and hillsides. She had never before seen so much snow. In Hertfordshire or in London, where she sometimes had spent a part of winter with the Gardiners, the snow appeared, but it was usually a light dusting, melting as soon as it fell. She was more accustomed to cold rain and wind in winter months.

The carriage rolled slowly, the coach seemingly well aware of the white fluff coating the road.

At last they emerged from the park and rolled onto the road leading directly to the front entrance of the house.

Elizabeth straightened her back, her hand running down her torso and legs, smoothing the new, elegant coat which Mrs. Bennet and Jane had selected for her during their stay in London.

"How do I look?" she asked her husband.

Darcy smiled reassuringly. "Perfect, Mrs. Darcy."

Elizabeth smiled back, but his support did little to take away from her overall nervousness. The servants at Pemberley, at least some of them, had already seen her last summer, but at the time she had been here in a completely different role.

She felt much recovered after the wedding night. For the last two nights Darcy had allowed her to sleep peacefully. They had kissed and embraced closely, but he did not try to initiate intimacy again. Elizabeth was much relieved and thankful for his consideration. Her backache was mostly gone. Even though the tenderness between her legs was still present, she could at least walk gracefully again.

At last the carriage stopped. The door opened and Darcy climbed out first before helping her down.

Instantly, Elizabeth felt the cold wind blowing straight into her face, taking her breath away. She shuddered, and Darcy must have noticed that because he whispered in her ear, "Let us hurry with it."

Elizabeth accepted his arm and they walked to greet the housekeeper, Mrs. Reynolds. Behind her there were two long rows of servants, women at the front with the men behind them.

Mrs. Reynolds welcomed them on behalf of herself and the rest of the staff. However, when she turned to introduce the servants to their new mistress, Darcy interrupted her, "Forgive me, Mrs. Reynolds, but further introductions can be done on a later date. I am sure that Mrs. Darcy will want to meet everyone personally. We are quite tired after a long journey.

Thank you all for your warm welcome," he spoke in the general direction of the crowd.

Elizabeth wondered if she should add something, but Darcy gave her little choice, pulling her inside. She hoped to walk with dignity, with her back straight and her steps well measured.

"We will take tea upstairs," Darcy said to Mrs. Reynolds as he helped Elizabeth out of her long coat, gloves and bonnet, passing it to the curvaceous woman standing close to them. Elizabeth wondered if it was her new maid, but she had no time to ask, as her husband took her arm, leading them away.

As they walked through the house, Elizabeth tried to recognize the familiar places, comparing it to the memories that she had stored from her summer visit. Darcy led her up to the grand staircase and into the family wing. They walked through darkened corridors until they reached a solid, massive door. Darcy pushed it open and they walked in.

"The sitting room, our bedroom, my room, and this small room shall be your dressing room," he explained, walking around and opening different doors. "Those rooms have not changed much since my mother's death. Everything was thoroughly cleaned and refreshed for us. The mattress, bedcovers, carpets and curtains were replaced, but you can redecorate it according to your own taste."

Elizabeth sat on the edge of the bed, gazing around the pale blue room.

"My mother liked pastel colours, but you may want to have it changed into a darker shade."

"It is lovely as it is," she assured him. The room was beautiful, but she was not certain if she would not wish to change it in the future. Nevertheless, she felt that it was too early to think about it.

Darcy sat next to her. "Are you well?"

She smiled. "Overwhelmed, perhaps."

With a smile of his own, he knelt down in front of her, removing her shoes and thick woollen stockings. His fingers kneaded her bare feet.

"Do you want to meet your lady's maid now?"

"Of course."

Darcy disappeared for a moment before returning with the same woman who was with them downstairs, the one who collected Elizabeth's belongings. "Mrs. Darcy, allow me to introduce Mrs. Pike."

Elizabeth smiled, nodding her head at the older woman, who in return dropped a proper curtsey.

"Mrs. Pike served as a lady's maid for a daughter of our close neighbour, Lady Harriet Cavendish, until she married and moved to London with her husband. Mrs. Pike did not wish to leave Derbyshire, as her children live here. Mrs. Reynolds was lucky to engage her with us."

Elizabeth smiled kindly at the older woman, who could easily be her mother.

"I will leave you now," Darcy said.

As she was alone with Mrs. Pike, Elizabeth did not quite know what to say to her. She had never had her own lady's maid, not to mention one who formerly served the duke's daughter.

The woman smiled brightly before speaking, "Would you care to change from your travelling clothes, Mrs. Darcy? I have pressed one of the day dresses for you."

"Yes, please," Elizabeth spoke. Elizabeth disrobed herself quickly as Mrs. Pike gathered her tall boots and stockings, which Darcy had abandoned on the floor earlier on. It was strange to have someone helping her with putting on a dress, but Elizabeth accepted the assistance graciously, not wishing to offend the woman.

Within minutes she was dressed in a lovely woollen gown with long sleeves in a rich yellow colour. Matching shoes made of thinnest leather were on her feet, and a blue knitted shawl around her arms.

"Shall we pin your hair again, my lady?" Mrs. Pike asked, causing Elizabeth to reach her hand to the simple bun she had twisted herself.

"I had no help this morning," Elizabeth explained herself, justifying the simplicity of her hairstyle.

"I understand, my lady. You did very well on your own."

Mrs. Pike unpinned her hair, brushing it in sure, well-measured strokes. "What lovely hair, so thick, long and shiny. It will be a joy to work with it. Naturally wavy too, no need to wear curling papers for the night."

"Thank you," Elizabeth said, watching in wonder as the woman quickly pinned the long sections of hair, creating an elaborate hairstyle. The most surprising was that she pulled Elizabeth's fringe back, revealing her high, smooth forehead.

"Do you wish me to leave some curls down your back?" Mrs. Pike asked. "They would look lovely on your long neck."

"I trust you," Elizabeth assured, curious what her lady's maid would do. She watched as Mrs. Pike released a few loose strands at the back, brushing them straight before curling them anew with hot pincers freshly taken away from the fireplace.

Elizabeth gaped at her reflection for the longest moment as the woman finished her task. She barely recognised herself. The new hairstyle made her look more mature, elegant, worldly and sophisticated; even her eyes seemed bigger. Gone was Lizzy Bennet. Some strange woman was looking back at her in the mirror.

"Elizabeth, dearest." She heard her husband's deep voice as Darcy entered the room. "You look beautiful," he shared his opinion, placing his hands on her arms. Elizabeth blushed, meeting his gaze.

"Excellent job, Mrs. Pike," Darcy praised. "I see that what Mrs. Reynolds told me about you was not in the least exaggerated."

"Thank you, Master," the woman answered calmly. "It is a pleasure to serve young Mrs. Darcy. Will you wish for a bath tonight, my lady?" the woman asked, turning her attention to Elizabeth.

"Yes, please, and thank you," Elizabeth responded. "You are very skilled. I barely recognised myself."

Mrs. Pike walked out, carrying Elizabeth's belongings in her arms.

"Do you like her?" Darcy asked.

"I do," she confirmed. "She seems kind, tactful and very helpful."

"Good. I am happy that you are pleased with her. Now come." He extended his arm to her. "The tea is waiting."

***

Elizabeth opened her eyes to the semidarkness created by the tightly drawn curtains around the four-poster bed. She rose on her elbow, reaching for the opening in the thick material. The bright daylight fell through the gap. She wondered what hour it was. She lay back, enjoying the feeling of love and contentment enveloping her like a cocoon. Her husband was pressed to her back, his strong thigh entwined with her legs, his arm draped over her midsection.

Not being able to return to sleep, she pried herself from Darcy's hold, mindful not to wake him, and climbed out of the bed. The fire was blazing in the fireplace, making the room comfortably warm despite the severe cold outside. She found her robe and slippers waiting for her on the nearest chair.

Last night they had stayed up quite late, talking and laughing. Darcy was in an excellent mood, happy to be back in his family home. They did not leave their rooms upstairs, and even had their dinner there.

Elizabeth found her way to the dressing room and tended to her necessities. She cleaned her face and teeth. Her brush and comb as well as other toiletries had been unpacked and laid down on top of the vanity.

"My lady, you are up!" She heard the surprised voice of Mrs. Pike. "Good morning."

"Good morning, Mrs. Pike. What time is it?"

"A quarter past seven. I thought that you would like to sleep in, being tired after the long journey from the south."

"I am not tired," Elizabeth assured.

The door opened and a very sleepy-looking Darcy, clad only in his long white nightshirt, stepped in. "Lizzy..." His dark eyes found his wife, smiling at her before settling on the other woman. "Mrs. Pike, good morning. Tell Wilkins to have my riding attire ready, and we will eat breakfast here, not downstairs." Then he stretched his arm towards Elizabeth, beckoning her to him. "Mrs. Darcy."

She walked to her husband, slightly surprised with his casual manner in front of the servant, who just then hastily left the room. Mrs. Pike, as Elizabeth's lady's maid, and Wilkins, Darcy's valet, were two people in the household who were the most closely involved in their everyday routine and the intimate side of their life and marriage. Perhaps it was the reason why Darcy was much less formal in their company.

"How did you sleep?" he asked.

"Very well."

"I am sorry to leave you alone, but I need to check those damages to the roof of the stables."

Elizabeth nodded. "I understand." Darcy had been informed yesterday that due to the heavy snowfall, the roof of the stables was endangered.

He put his hands on her waist, gazing into her eyes. "I should spend your first day at Pemberley with you."

"I shall be very well on my own, Fitzwilliam. I should begin learning the names of the servants and discuss household matters with Mr. Reynolds."

"There is no hurry for that. You should rest today. In the afternoon I will show you more of the house. During your last visit you saw only the parts that we show to tourists."

"I would prefer to meet the servants today," Elizabeth insisted.

"Are you certain?"

"Absolutely," she answered. She wished to show Darcy that her intention was to treat her new role as the mistress of Pemberley with responsibility and devotion. She was prepared to work hard in order to make a difference as the new Mrs. Darcy.

"Very well. Tell Mrs. Pike to ask Mrs. Reynolds to assemble all the servants in the great hall at nine. I will introduce you to the staff. They should be aware that you have my full support."

"Thank you, Fitzwilliam."

"But remember, the afternoon belongs to me. It is our honeymoon, after all. You will have plenty of opportunity to look into the household affairs."

***

Darcy walked her to the great hall but did not stay there with her for long. He was in a hurry to see the damages done to the stables with his own eyes. Elizabeth was left alone with Mrs. Reynolds and nearly fifty servants looking at her curiously.

It took nearly an hour to have all of them introduced. The housekeeper gave the name of every person and shortly explained their occupation in the house. Elizabeth listened intently, trying to remember as many of them as possible.

After the introductions were made, she stepped back and spoke in a firm, calm voice, "I would like to thank you all for such a gracious welcome. I do hope that we shall work together for the good of Pemberley. If you wish to address me personally, do not be afraid to approach me. However, Mrs. Reynolds, as the housekeeper, should be addressed first with all the troubling matters." She took a moment to look into their faces. "Thank you. You may return to your work."

"Do you wish to see the household accounts now, Mrs. Darcy?" Mrs. Reynolds enquired as the servants hastily scurried away.

"Not today. I promised Mr. Darcy that we would spend the afternoon together."

"Very well, Mistress."

Elizabeth smiled at the older woman. Darcy spoke very highly about the housekeeper. He seemed very attached to her. Georgiana also mentioned her often. Elizabeth wished for the woman's approval of her person.

"I am very curious of the grounds," she confessed. "Especially now when everything is covered with snow. We barely have any snow in the south; mostly it rains in winter. Even when it does snow it melts away almost instantly."

"This year's winter is proving to be quite harsh in Derbyshire. Here at Pemberley it is always colder than in the south of the country."

Elizabeth walked to the window, glancing at the snow-covered courtyard. "I would like to walk to the stables to meet Mr. Darcy there."

"I will send the footman with you to show you the way," Mrs. Reynolds suggested.

"Excellent. I am afraid I would have trouble finding the way by myself."

Half an hour later, Elizabeth, wrapped up in the long coat lined with fur, with tall boots with thick soles on her legs, was trotting through the snow towards the stables. She found Darcy right in front of the long, handsome building, talking to several men. On seeing her, he abandoned their company, hurrying in her direction.

"Has something happened?" were his first words.

"You said that we would spend the afternoon together," she reminded him. "I decided to meet you here."

"I am pleased, my dearest. However, on such a cold day, you should have stayed home."

Elizabeth was quite warm apart from her face and the tip of her nose, which felt like a piece of ice, and she told him so, adding brightly, "The grounds are breathtaking with the frozen lake and frosted trees."

Her assertions did not calm him. "Nevertheless, you are not accustomed to such harsh conditions. It would be for the best to return home immediately."

With reluctance, Elizabeth accepted his arm and they walked back home.

CHAPTER NINETEEN

Elizabeth walked into the bedroom dressed for the night, her hair braided down her back. Mrs. Pike continued to be a delight. She was most helpful but also very tactful. Even when Elizabeth asked to have prepared the see-through nightgown, the gift from Aunt Gardiner, Mrs. Pike did not even bat an eyelid, but did exactly what she had been asked to do. Elizabeth had no doubt that she would adjust very quickly to the comfort of having a maid to her own disposal.

She sat close to the fireplace, enjoying the warmth coming from it. She had to admit that Darcy had been correct on saying how much colder Pemberley was when compared to Longbourn or London. As they had walked through the house today, Darcy giving her the private tour of the parts of the house which she had not seen previously, the chill ran down her back more than once despite her warm, woollen dress and a thick shawl around her shoulders.

Darcy must have crept into the room like a cat, because Elizabeth was not aware of his presence until she felt a hand on her shoulder and soft lips on her cheek.

"How are you, dearest?" he asked, kneeling next to her.

"I am well."

He took a seat on a chair, facing her, leaning forward. "I wish for you to be happy here."

"I am, I will be."

"You left your home, family, Jane, your father, the Gardiners. I expect you to feel homesick and lonely, especially in the first months."

She reached to touch his knee. "I have not had time to feel homesick yet. As for loneliness, I have you."

"Nevertheless, remember that I am here to assist you in any way I can."

Elizabeth's response to his words was a kiss. Soon she was moved to sit on his lap as his hands stroked down her arms, sides and legs.

"Have you recovered?" he enquired, nibbling at her neck.

"Recovered?" she repeated distractedly, enjoying his caresses too much to pay attention to what he was saying.

He stopped his ministrations and pulled back slightly to look her in the eye. "I do realize that I was quite demanding on our wedding night."

With a smile, Elizabeth rose to her feet, standing in front of him with her back to the fireplace. With quick fingers she untied her robe, allowing it to fall to the ground.

Darcy's dark eyes roamed over her body clad in a sheer shift as he murmured in a thick voice, "I guess that our thoughts and desires have gone in the same direction this evening. Did your aunt give you only this one nightgown, or perhaps you have a couple more similar ones?"

"Only this one."

"You should purchase more. I would welcome you wearing one of these every night."

"It is not the most comfortable attire," she whispered. "I much prefer the usual simple cotton shifts."

Darcy put his hands on her hips, drawing her closer to him. "Then I insist on removing it." He stood to his full height, his fingers gathering the thin material and lifting it up over her head, removing it completely. "My dearest, loveliest Elizabeth."

Quickly they found their way to bed. Elizabeth enjoyed his ardent kisses as he pulled her underneath her in the security of his strong embrace. She relaxed under his gentle touch, especially enjoying the attention he gave the sensitive skin of her inner thighs.

She was most astonished, however, when her husband suddenly rolled them over so that he was on his back and she was perched on his waist, with her legs curled awkwardly on his sides. She placed her open palms on the wide plains of his chest, unsure what to do next and what was expected from her.

"It should feel far more pleasurable for you this way," he explained, keeping her firmly in place, his hands on her waist.

"Fitzwilliam?" she enquired unsurely.

One of his hands left her side to cup her cheek. "You are considerably shorter than I. It has been a long time since I began to consider how to love you so we could see eye to eye."

"Since how long?"

"Very long," he assured. "Come, kiss me."

She leaned down, touching her lips with his. His hand on her hip pressed her down onto him, while his other hand cupped her breast, his thumb teasing the tip.

"Move with me," he encouraged.

"I cannot," she stammered, avoiding looking into his eyes. She was embarrassed. She distinctively felt his hardness pressing in her. He could see her clearly in all her nudity. It was too much to bear.

He was not upset with her denial, but he changed his own position, sitting up, still cradling her to him, only now they were face to face, their chests touching. She hid her face in the crook of his neck as he stroked her back, guiding her movements with his hand on her bottom.

Elizabeth gasped as he slipped inside of her body. They moved together for a moment, face to face, Elizabeth adjusting to the new sensations. She had to admit that this unusual position was indeed far more pleasurable to what she had experienced before. Soon enough she stopped caring whether he could see her naked and vulnerable, and she was moving with him, throwing her head back and moaning loudly. She must have bit down on his shoulder in the moment of greatest passion, but she only realized it when she collapsed on top of him, boneless and sweaty.

It was quite a long time before her heart stopped hammering in her chest. Darcy did nothing to remove her from him, only covered them both with a sheet. His hand was stroking her bare back repeatedly, reaching from her shoulder blade to her thigh and repeating the motion many times all over again.

The thought crossed her mind that her Fitzwilliam seemed to be much more knowledgeable about matters of the flesh than she would have expected him to be. She was not naive enough to believe that a man of his age, experience and position could be entirely innocent. He had been to university; he had had opportunity to travel abroad. But foremost, he was a man, not a sheltered young girl raised in the country like her. During their engagement he had told her much about his life, but he never mentioned any previous love interests. Did it mean that he had none? The way he touched her was a testimony to his worldliness in that respect, especially in Elizabeth's eyes. He knew exactly what to do, there was no hesitation, not a trace of fumbling in his moves, kisses and embraces.

"Are you asleep?" he enquired, touching her cheek to make her look at him.

Elizabeth caught his gaze with her own. "I was thinking,"

she admitted.

Gently, he shifted them so she lay down on her side, facing him. "About?" he asked, searching her eyes.

"That you are a kind man and very good to me."

He smiled boyishly. "I do hope so. Your good opinion is of utmost importance to me."

Elizabeth snuggled closer into his arms as he covered her with an additional woollen blanket. Her husband was the best of men. His past did not bother her, even though it was self-evident to her that he had loved another one or even other ones before her. She trusted him. He would have told her himself if there had been the slightest reason for her to worry about the women from his past.

***

The first weeks of her marriage passed quickly, with Elizabeth adjusting well to her life as Mrs. Darcy. Everything was new and exciting, beginning from the change in her daily routine and ending on the fact that her nights were at least partially sleepless. Her honest plans to undertake the duties of the mistress of Pemberley with seriousness and devotion were often interrupted, postponed, or even cancelled. Her husband was the one who demanded her attention the most.

To Elizabeth's disappointment, the beautiful snow which welcomed her to Pemberley melted away, and it began to rain heavily. It was cold and windy, which forbade her from exploring the grounds. Nevertheless, Darcy was quite resourceful at filling their days with pleasurable activities, even when they were restricted to staying indoors. Mrs. Reynolds was asked to inform any possible visitors, mainly neighbours who wanted to pay a visit to the newlyweds, that Mr. and Mrs. Darcy were currently away and not admitting anyone.

In the years to come, Elizabeth would often return to the memories of her first month of marriage with great fondness. She remembered it as a time when she was all alone with her husband, sleeping late, laughing, chasing around the house and playing silly games behind the closed doors of the library without the fear of being seen by anyone. They were not interrupted by social obligations, the relatives, or their own children. In Elizabeth's view, it was an ideal honeymoon, even though it was freezing cold and it rained constantly.

***

"You have received a letter from Jane?" Darcy enquired, entering their private sitting room.

"No, from Charlotte Lucas," she responded. She was curled on the cushioned seat in the wide bow window. So far it was her favourite spot to read in the entire house. Not only was the light excellent, but also there was a beautiful view of the lake, park, and hills behind it.

Darcy took a seat on the other end of the window, pulling her feet over onto his lap. "What did she write?"

"She gave birth to twins, a baby girl and a boy, three weeks ago. She is recovering well while the babies are healthy and beautiful. They named them Catherine Elizabeth and William Richard. She writes that she would prefer Elizabeth to be the first name for a girl, but her husband insisted on Catherine. Charlotte is relieved that the children do not resemble Mr. Collins in the least. They have fine, pale blonde hair and large blue eyes."

Darcy tickled the sole of her feet, to which she tried to pull away her legs, but he stopped her with a steady grasp on her ankles. "I am not surprised that they do not resemble Collins," he said.

"When it comes to such tiny little ones, it is impossible to decide about such matters, as the features are only beginning to shape. I remember my cousins when they were that age. It was impossible to decide for certain whether they looked like Aunt Madeline or Uncle Edward until they were at least four or five months old."

"What I meant to say is that Mrs. Collins may have reasons to believe that the children will certainly not resemble her husband."

Elizabeth's eyes locked on Darcy's profile as he tried to tickle her feet again.

"What is your meaning?"

Darcy shrugged his broad shoulders. "Nothing of

consequence."

With a decided tug, Elizabeth freed her legs from his hold only to kneel beside him. "You know something," she stated. She cupped his cheek to make him look into her eyes. "Tell me."

Darcy shook his head. "I should not have mentioned anything," he murmured.

"But you did. Now finish. Please."

"It is simple enough. I have reasons to believe that your cousin is not the father of little Catherine Elizabeth and William Richard."

"Who is it, then?"

"Can you not guess?"

Elizabeth frowned heavily. "I cannot. There were hardly any men at Rosings or Hunsford last spring when the twins had to be begotten. You do not think that it could be some servant or your aunt's steward? That I will not believe."

"Elizabeth, truly, there were men at Rosings Park last spring."

Elizabeth sat back, staring at him imploringly. "Colonel Fitzwilliam," she whispered, her voice no more than a whisper.

Darcy breathed out in relief. "I am glad that you have not accused me of the deed."

Elizabeth rolled her eyes. "I do believe that at the time you were far more occupied with me to even look elsewhere." She leaned back to him, touching his arm. “How do you know about it? Did Colonel Fitzwilliam confide in you?”

“God forbid. I saw them one day.”

“Where? What did you see?”

“In the forest. There is an abandoned hut there, we played there as children together with Anne.”

“I remember. I walked by it a few times on my daily walks but I never saw anyone in there. Perhaps you are mistaken, perhaps they were only talking.”

“Believe me, dearest, they were doing much more than just talking. You remember how we witnessed Bingley leaving Jane’s bedroom that night at Netherfield? What I saw was very much of the same nature.”

“It is the reason why you were so jealous over Colonel Fitzwilliam?”

“Perhaps. After all, the marriage vows did not stop him from seducing your friend.”

“I am not certain that it was him who seduced her. It might have been Charlotte who initiated that.”

Darcy watched her closely. “You do not seem particularly offended with such a possibility.”

“I am not. If I were married to a man like Mr. Collins, I would not wish to share his bed, nor to have a child with him.” She put her arms around his neck. “If I were in Charlotte’s position, I would seduce you, Mr. Darcy. At least, I would try.”

He pulled her to him, sitting her on his lap. "Do not even mention the possibility of being married to another man, especially such a silly one like your cousin. Nevertheless, I am pleased to hear that you would choose to seduce me and not my cousin."

Elizabeth settled into his embrace, quieting down, many thoughts running through her head. She could hardly blame Charlotte for what she had done. Colonel Fitzwilliam was a handsome, kind, gentle, and intelligent man, not to mention that he was impeccably dressed and took a bath at least once every few days. All that could not be said about Mr. Collins.

"What are your thoughts, dearest?" Darcy asked, kissing her temple.

"I should send a present for the babies."

"You should," he agreed.

"Do you think that Colonel Fitzwilliam knows about it?"

"He may not be aware. I cannot imagine that he and Mrs. Collins keep correspondence. I do not believe that he writes to Lady Catherine either. My guess is that he does not know. He will learn about it eventually."

"Will you tell him when he comes here with Georgiana?"

Darcy was silent for a moment longer. "I probably should mention it to him, and also make him aware that I know of the children's true parentage. In this situation I am not certain if I would want him to marry Georgiana. After all that happened with George Wickham, she does not deserve a husband who has out-of-wedlock children with a married woman. Let us hope that Georgiana will not take a fancy to Colonel Fitzwilliam after all. We must introduce some decent young men to her once she is eighteen. She should have a choice."

"I am not certain what to think of Colonel Fitzwilliam's conduct, but as for Charlotte, I am truly happy for her."

"You are?"

"She has beautiful little twins with a man she liked, if not loved."

"What about Mr. Collins? Should we not pity him?"

"He deserves it," Elizabeth spoke firmly. "I could never find any goodness in him."

Darcy groaned loudly, hiding his face in her throat. "I do not look forward to facing Colonel Fitzwilliam when he brings Georgiana home in two days' time."

"You must," she said, gently tugging at his brown locks. "Especially if he seriously considers marrying Georgiana in a few years. Colonel Fitzwilliam should know that he fathered not one child but two."

"There still might be a possibility that the twins are Collins's."

"There is," Elizabeth agreed, "but I doubt it. Charlotte is clever. She kept her husband at arm's length and she told me herself that they spent very little time together. They had separate bedrooms. During my stay at Hunsford, my room was next to Charlotte's, and I never heard anything indicating that he paid her nightly visits."

Darcy sighed, kissing her neck. "I do not envy my cousin, but he is not some youth. He knew what he was doing. He should have thought about the consequences of his actions."

CHAPTER TWENTY

From the corner of her eye, Elizabeth watched her husband talking with Colonel Fitzwilliam, their fine figures cut sharply against the light coming from the fireplace. Darcy's expression was neutral, but Colonel Fitzwilliam's forehead was drawn into a heavy frown. She could only assume that Darcy had just mentioned to his cousin of Mrs. Collins giving birth to a baby girl and boy almost exactly nine months after his departure from Kent.

Elizabeth turned her attention to Georgiana, not wishing the gentlemen to guess that she was observing them.

Her new sister was giving her a detailed account of her stay with her aunt and uncle, Earl and Countess of Matlock, at Matlock Hall. "Everyone at Matlock is so very much pleased that Henrietta is with child," the girl said.

"Lady Henrietta is the wife of the elder brother of Colonel Fitzwilliam, am I correct?" Elizabeth asked.

"Indeed she is. The Matlocks hope for a boy."

"The heir to the name, title and the lands," Elizabeth guessed. "I can understand that very well. There will be no more Bennets in Herdforshire, as I have no brother."

"Still, the child may be a girl," Georgiana mused. "There is no certainty on such matters."

"True. And if the child proves to be another girl, then the responsibility for continuity of the family name will rest solely on Colonel Fitzwilliam."

As she said the words, Elizabeth watched Georgiana closely, searching for any clues indicating that the girl was aware of the possible match between her and Colonel Fitzwilliam, but she found nothing. Her lovely face was calm and unassuming.

"Not exactly," Georgiana answered.

Elizabeth frowned slightly. "No? Are there some distant cousins to be taken into consideration?" she asked, thinking of Mr. Collins, who was to inherit Longbourn.

"Brother will inherit the title if both Colonel Fitzwilliam and Lord Castlereagh do not have sons."

Elizabeth's eyes flew across the room to her husband. "Fitzwilliam?"

"Naturally. Our mother was the daughter of the Earl of Matlock," Georgiana reminded her. "The daughter of the earl cannot directly inherit the title, but her son certainly can. It is certain that Uncle would prefer for his grandson to carry on the family name. Nevertheless, I cannot imagine him to be upset if it were Brother who would be the next earl. Brother is an excellent man, he would never bring shame or disgrace to the family and family name."

Georgiana changed the topic then, confessing to Elizabeth

that the pianoforte at Matlock Hall was quite old and not as good as the instrument she had at Pemberley. Elizabeth proposed that Georgiana should play for the company. Her sister agreed, but only on the condition that Elizabeth sing.

Darcy welcomed the idea of a concert from his ladies with great enthusiasm, while Colonel Fitzwilliam bowed his head, being visibly distracted.

As Elizabeth sang, her eyes rested more than once on Colonel Fitzwilliam. His expression was as flat and disinterested as never before. She was convinced now that her husband had indeed told him the news of his possible fatherhood.

***

"What did he say?" Elizabeth enquired as soon as her husband entered their bedroom.

"You are not asleep?" Darcy asked. "It is late." He quickly removed his clothing, discarding the items carelessly on a nearby chair.

"What was Colonel Fitzwilliam's reaction to the news?"

Darcy cocked his eyebrow. "What news?"

Elizabeth threw a pillow at him with all her might. "Do not tease me, Fitzwilliam Darcy." She glared at him.

He put the pillow back against the headboard before climbing under the covers naked as a newborn babe.

"Well?" Elizabeth pressed, very agitated. "Did you tell him? I can only guess that you did, but he was absentminded till the very end of the evening."

"I presented the matter to him succinctly," Darcy admitted. "However, he said nothing about it."

"Nothing, nothing at all?"

"Almost nothing. When he enquired about how you are liking Pemberley and if you are not feeling lonely here, I told him that you receive many letters on a daily basis from your family and friends. Then I mentioned the news of twins, boy and a girl, being born to your friend Mrs. Collins."

"And?"

"He asked about the exact date of the birth, and I told him that he would have to ask you about the details, but that the happy event took place in the beginning of January."

Elizabeth leaned back against the pillows. "He did ask about the birth date," she whispered. "Then he must have considered the possibility of being the father."

"Possibly," Darcy agreed. "He was unusually quiet for the rest of the evening. You noticed it."

She nodded. "I certainly did."

"When he wished to stay in the library for a drink after you and Georgiana retired, I thought that he intended to speak to me, to seek advice perhaps."

"But he did not," Elizabeth guessed.

"He did not," he confirmed. "He was mostly silent and

drank very little, barely half the glass of the brandy, which is a favourite of his."

"I observed him carefully throughout the evening. He was very distracted, not his usual jovial self."

"We cannot do much more on the matter, I am afraid."

Elizabeth leaned against his chest, thinking for a moment longer. Darcy was silent as well. His arms came around her, and he kissed the top of her head.

"What will Colonel Fitzwilliam do next? Will he contact Charlotte? What is your opinion?" she enquired, turning her head to look into Darcy's face.

"Even if he is the father, he cannot do much about it."

"He must be," Elizabeth insisted. "I am convinced about it."

"It is better for Catherine Elizabeth and William Richard to be known as Miss Collins and Mr. Collins in the future, the daughter and son of a parson, rather than the illegitimate children of the second son of the Earl of Matlock."

"That is true," Elizabeth agreed quietly. She shifted in his embrace, placing her head on his chest, her fingers stroking the fine hair covering his chest. "Poor Charlotte," she breathed.

"Poor? I daresay that she knew very well what she was doing. My cousin did not coerce her into anything she did not want. I am not even certain who seduced whom."

"Judging from Charlotte's letter, she is very happy with the birth of her children. What I meant to say is that she cannot enjoy her little girl and boy together with the children's father by her side."

"What about my cousin? He will never be able to acknowledge his own daughter and son, or even see them more than a few times during her lifetime."

"Georgiana mentioned to me that the Matlocks anticipate the birth of yet another grandchild."

"Indeed. Colonel Fitzwilliam explained to me that they were not announcing it for a long time, fearing another miscarriage. Lady Henrietta's condition has become visible only in the last weeks, and they trust that this time she will carry the baby safely to the end."

"They hope for a boy."

Darcy nodded. "The boy would dissolve many concerns for all of them. Colonel Fitzwilliam would not feel pressured to marry within the next year or two. I doubt that he is willing to seriously consider marriage now, especially with the news coming from Kent."

Elizabeth rose on her elbow, staring into his eyes. "Georgiana told me that you will inherit the title if both Colonel Fitzwilliam and Lord Castlereagh fail to produce the heir."

"The possibility is so slight that I have never truly considered it."

"Perhaps it is the reason why the earl and countess were so

kind to me and so supportive of our union. They wished to see you married, with the possibility of having children of your own."

"Uncle is very proud of his ancestry and the family name. He is the fifth Earl of Matlock, and he does not wish for his sons to be the last to carry on the title. But if, as you said, they fail to produce sons, I can imagine him welcoming our son as his heir." With those words, Darcy frowned, and he watched his wife through narrowed eyes. "Dearest," he said, reaching his hand to touch her cheek. "Do you have something to announce to me?"

"Not yet."

"Oh?"

"I am not certain yet. My monthly courses should have come three weeks ago."

He grinned. "You are with child, then?"

"It is too soon to tell, Fitzwilliam."

He pushed her on her back, looming over her, his hand finding his way to her waist, pressing there. "How are you feeling?"

"Very well."

His eyes grew darker with concern. "Are you certain?"

She combed her fingers through his locks. "It is too early to experience any discomfort."

"A physician should see you," he insisted firmly.

"I am well, Fitzwilliam. We must wait and see."

"Then a midwife, perhaps," he proposed. "Mrs. Gibbs, who delivered Georgiana, is well and working. She lives in Lambton."

Elizabeth considered his offer but she shook her head. "People will guess instantly when they learn that I met her, unless she steals here at night. Let us wait until I feel the quickening."

"When will it happen?"

"In a few months, I imagine."

Darcy pulled her to him, his arms around her wounding so tightly that it was almost painful and difficult to take a deeper breath. "I must take good care of you now, Mrs. Darcy."

"You are always very attentive to me, Fitzwilliam," she assured.

He squeezed her to him, gentler this time. "I did not expect for it to happen so soon. The baby."

She yawned, snuggling against him. "You are pleased with the possibility."

"'Pleased' is too mild a word. So much happiness, Elizabeth. Sometimes I can barely believe it."

***

The spring came rather late that year. Only with the beginning of April did the weather improve enough to enjoy longer walks. It was still cold, but at least the torrential rains ceased. Elizabeth was most pleased because both her father and Jane were coming for a visit. It had been over three months since she had seen them, and she missed them dearly. She was quite astonished that her mother did not wish to join them to see Pemberley for the first time. The letter from Jane explained the reason behind Mrs. Bennet's decision to stay behind in Hertfordshire. Apparently, there was a young man back at home who was courting Mary. He was from Bedfordshire, the owner of a modest estate giving little less than one thousand pounds of yearly income. Mrs. Bennet found him quite suitable for Mary even though he did not keep his own carriage. Nevertheless, the mother of five daughters, three of who were already safely married, had no intention to leave Longbourn until Mary was spoken for, preferably married.

Elizabeth awaited the arrival of her family with great hopes. Her initial idea that Mr. Bingley should buy the estate in the north seemed more likely to happen with every passing month. Through Jane's letters she learned that the Bingleys were already tired with the close proximity to the Bennet family, especially since Mrs. Bennet considered it to be her duty to visit Netherfield every single day, finding it necessary to advise the newly married on numerous matters. Now was the perfect time to present to her sister and her husband the proposition of moving to the north of the country, preferably to

Derbyshire or any other neighbouring county. Darcy had already been properly instructed to make the suggestion to his friend that settling away from Hertfordshire was a worthy concept. After all, Mr. Bingley had always taken Darcy's advice into serious consideration. Elizabeth could already see the near future with Jane living not more than a day away from Pemberley.

CHAPTER TWENTY- ONE

Darcy walked through the house, his long legs carrying him in the direction of the drawing room. He was quite certain he would find his wife and sister there. But as he entered, he saw only Georgiana, hunched over some music sheets.

"Have you seen Elizabeth?" he asked. "I thought that we were having tea together."

Georgiana looked up. "She went out to look for the carriage."

Darcy frowned, glancing out of the window. "She should have stayed. It might begin to rain any moment."

"She looks forward to seeing her sister and father. She said that she could not sit here calmly when they were expected at any moment."

"I will bring her back. The roads are still in a bad state; the Bingleys will surely come late, perhaps even tomorrow."

"You do that, Brother," she said, smiling.

Darcy shook his head, noticing the twinkle in his sister's eyes. Georgiana had been recently borrowing some of Elizabeth's expressions and mannerisms. He leaned over to kiss her glossy blonde hair. "Light up the candles," he told her. "You will ruin your eyesight reading without light on such a cloudy day."

"Yes, Brother."

As he stepped out of the front entrance, he looked around, hoping to find his wife there, but he was not successful. With a sigh he strode quickly along the road leading through the park directly to Lambton. There he saw her small figure ambling up the hill.

"Elizabeth!" he cried out.

She turned around, waving at him. Darcy hurried his pace, signalling so she would stay in place.

"What are you doing here?" he demanded in his first words.

"Jane and Papa should have already arrived. I thought I would look out for them."

"It is cold and getting dark. Come, let us go back."

Elizabeth turned her head towards the bend in the road, rising on her tiptoes and squinting her eyes in hope of seeing the carriage. With a resigned sigh, she accepted her husband's offered arm after a moment.

"You felt so unwell this morning. You should have stayed home today," he fretted.

"I am well now. The sickness goes away later in the day. Mrs. Pike always knows how to help me at such times."

"I am simply concerned about you, your health and our child's wellbeing."

She stopped walking and turned sideways to face him.

"Fitzwilliam, I am truly very well. I am young and healthy. Strong, too," she spoke evenly. "I understand that you are hunted with the memories of your mother, how she suffered through her many miscarriages. However, let me remind you one more time: My mother gave birth to five healthy babies in less than ten years and she is still in excellent health."

He wrapped his arms around her, placing her head on his chest. He could not even think that something might happen to Elizabeth or their baby. He had been old enough to understand why his mother had been bedridden so often before Georgiana's birth.

"Everything is well," she assured him again, her voice muffled against his coat.

After a moment they began to walk again, this time holding hands like small children.

"When are we going to announce the news about the impending birth of the new heir to Pemberley?" Darcy asked in a casual tone, but with a note of pride in his voice.

"Do we have to announce anything?" Elizabeth asked. "I am certain that many people have already guessed it. Soon enough my condition will be visible to everyone. In a month or two, I will not be able to hide it."

Naturally, Darcy could already see the changes in her body, but only when they were alone in the privacy of their bedroom. "Have you informed your mother?"

Elizabeth shook her head. "I have not. I feared that she would like to come here upon hearing the news despite Mary's possible engagement to that gentleman from Bedfordshire."

"I trust that you will tell Jane."

"I believe that Jane will guess on her own once she sees me. She can read me well."

"What about your father?"

"What about him?"

"Will he welcome the news?"

"Why should he not?"

Darcy hesitated with the answer. "You are his favourite. I doubt that he expected that he would become a grandfather so very soon."

"I guess that he will be pleased if he has a grandson. He always wished for a son."

As they reached the front entrance to the house, Elizabeth turned again, looking towards the road. "I am becoming worried. They should have arrived a few hours ago."

"They will be here tomorrow. They must have been delayed on the way. Bingley's coachman is experienced. There is nothing to fear."

Elizabeth sighed, her expression worried. "I hope so."

Placing his hand on her waist, he said, "I beg you not to worry. They will be here sooner than you think."

***

"Jane!" Elizabeth exclaimed, running into her sister's open arms. "I lost hope that you would arrive today."

"We were delayed because of a fallen tree on the road. Charles wished to stay at Lambton for the night, but I convinced him that we should drive straight to Pemberley," Jane explained, returning the embrace.

"Papa!" Elizabeth cried, moving to greet her father.

"My Lizzy," Mr. Bennet said, his voice thick with emotion.

As Elizabeth was greeting her family, Darcy walked to Bingley, who was left behind the company. They shook hands. "It is good to see you, Bingley," Darcy said, patting his friend's arm. "I can see that married life suits you well."

"Can I say the same about you?"

Darcy laughed. "You certainly can."

"I wanted to stay overnight at Lambton, but Jane could not stand the thought of not seeing her sister for one more night. I did not have the heart to refuse her."

"I understand you perfectly well, my friend. Elizabeth was guarding the road to Lambton for most of the afternoon, looking out for your carriage. With great effort I convinced her that she should wait inside."

Suddenly Bingley's expression turned uncharacteristically serious. "Darcy, I have to speak with you," he said in a lowered voice. "There is a serious matter we need to discuss. In private."

Darcy frowned. He had rarely seen Bingley as such. "Naturally. After Mr. Bennet and the ladies retire for the night, we shall talk in the library."

"Good, good. Excellent," Bingley murmured, moving to stand beside his wife.

Darcy stepped to greet his father-in-law now that Elizabeth had released Mr. Bennet from her embrace. He was very curious about what serious business Bingley had to discuss with him.

***

Darcy gave Bingley a glass of scotch as they sat by the fire in the library. "Well? What is the matter?"

His friend took a large gulp.

"Has something happened?" Darcy probed. "Problems? You need advice?"

Bingley shook his head. "No."

"Speak, then!" Darcy cried encouragingly.

Bingley looked him right in the eyes. "Caroline wants to see both you and Mrs. Darcy."

Darcy's expression fell, a frown marking his forehead. "Your sister?"

Bingley nodded.

"How is she feeling?" Darcy enquired. "You have not mentioned her much in your recent letters."

"She is very well, very well indeed. She feels ashamed of her past behaviour towards you and Mrs. Darcy. She wishes to speak to both of you and apologize."

Darcy leaned back in the armchair, raising his fist to his mouth. "Bingley, I will be honest with you. Elizabeth does not want to see Caroline, of that I am certain. I do not wish to upset my wife."

"Caroline is here."

"Here? At Pemberley?"

"She came with us but stayed behind. She is at the inn in Lambton. She understands that you may not want to host her."

"Why did she come here in the first place?" Darcy enquired angrily. "She was not invited."

"You must remember how stubborn she can be. She insists on apologizing to you and Elizabeth."

Darcy stood up. "Bingley, you are my friend, but Elizabeth is my dearest wife. I will do nothing to upset her. I do not care if your sister wants to clear her consciousness. I am pleased for her recovery, but she is no longer welcomed at Pemberley."

"Will you talk to Mrs. Darcy about it at the very least?"

Darcy hesitated. "I cannot promise anything."

"I understand. Thank you. Thank you, Darcy."

Darcy nodded but said nothing more. He valued Bingley's friendship, even more now when they were married to sisters. Nevertheless, his wife's wellbeing was of the most importance to him. In her delicate condition, Elizabeth was overly sensitive and emotional. He had no intention to allow Caroline Bingley to come to Pemberley if it meant upsetting his wife.

***

Elizabeth watched her husband from the corner of her eye. He had clearly been upset about some matter since last evening. She guessed that it was his conversation with his friend that had brought this change. She wondered what Bingley had said to him. They had shut themselves inside the library for quite some time after everyone had retired last night.

"What are your plans for today?" she asked, coming to stand next to Darcy as he was adjusting his cravat in front of the mirror. She leaned against him, touching her cheek to the sleeve of his white shirt.

He glanced down at her. "We have guests. I am pleased to see Bingley and your father. I look forward to spending some time in their company. I want to ask their opinion on the plans for the new stable."

Elizabeth locked her eyes with his, waiting for him to say more. He wished to share something with her, she could see it in his eyes and expression. "Is there something you wish to discuss with me?" she enquired at last.

Darcy turned to face her. "There might be."

"Might be?"

"It is not my intention to keep matters secret from you, but at the same time I wish to spare you unnecessary concern and worry."

"It must be something that Mr. Bingley told you last evening."

"It is."

"Well?" Elizabeth asked, feeling more and more impatient. She did not appreciate being kept in the dark. Jane as well seemed upset, but refused to confess anything. Were the Bingleys in trouble? Did they need their help?

"I talked with Bingley about his sister," Darcy blurted out at last.

"His sister? Mrs. Hurst?"

Darcy shook his head.

"Caroline? Is she sick again?"

"On the contrary. Miss Bingley is at Lambton. She wishes to speak with us. She wants to apologize to you and me."

Elizabeth stepped back from him. "I do not need her to apologize to me," she said.

Darcy nodded. "Very well. I will repeat that to Bingley."

Elizabeth began pacing the room, her steps becoming faster and more agitated with every second. "She should not have come here! We invited Jane, Mr. Bingley and Papa, certainly not her."

"I will tell Bingley that we will not see her."

"I do not trust her."

"Neither do I."

"If she wished to apologize, she should have written a letter."

Darcy caught her arm, stopping her in place. He drew her to him, placing his hands on her shoulders. "She will not come here. You are Mrs. Darcy and it is your decision who is invited to our home. Try to forget that I ever mentioned it. Remember about the babe. Your agitation is not good for it." One of his hands moved to her midsection. "I should have told Bingley straight away that his sister is not welcome here."

"I would not wish for you to hide this from me," she said, her voice and expression calmer.

He nodded. "I guessed as much."

Elizabeth squared her shoulders, lifting her chin. "It seems that we have plans for this morning after all. Ask for the carriage to be prepared. We are going to Lambton."

"We? You wish to speak to her after all?"

"Caroline Bingley wishes to apologize. Very well. I will allow her that courtesy. Later she can return to where she came from. I want to enjoy my family's visit. I do not see it possible with her in the company."

"I will go alone," Darcy offered. "I do not wish for you to become even more upset."

"To be completely truthful, I am not in the mood to see her."

"You have me, dearest, to help you and protect you. It is my right and duty. I do not trust Caroline Bingley. Charles thinks that she feels better and that she regrets her bad behaviour, but I remember all too well how she acted the last time she saw you. I will not take more risks."

"Will you go to see her all alone, then?"

"I will ask Bingley to join me. He will be my witness. Miss Bingley might be tempted to fabricate some details of our meeting if I talk to her alone."

Elizabeth smiled. "Very well, Fitzwilliam. Thank you, my knight in shining armour."

After such words, not much was left for him but to kiss her with all his love and devotion.

***

The meeting in Lambton with Caroline was short. Bingley and Darcy met her at the inn in the private room downstairs. Darcy explained that although Elizabeth and he accepted her apology and wished her all the best, she was not welcome at Pemberley. Caroline was silent. Darcy said his goodbyes quickly. He left Bingley behind alone with his sister, hurrying to see his wife.

Later that day he learned from Bingley that Caroline would be returning to London the following day. Darcy welcomed the news with relief. He sincerely hoped that it was the last time his friend's sister attempted to make contact with their family.

EPILOGUE

Elizabeth closed her eyes against the bright sunlight, enjoying the warmth on her face. The beautiful summer had almost ended, and she was determined to enjoy the last sunny days. It was becoming more and more difficult for her to move, and she preferred to sit on the terrace. Not to mention that her husband was beside himself with worry every time he saw her going for a walk. The midwife had said to her a week ago that the baby could be born any day. Since then, Darcy had been watching her like a hawk.

She heard the familiar steps coming from the house but she did not open her eyes, pretending to sleep.

A large, warm hand touched her face shortly before resting on her enlarged midsection.

Opening one eye, she saw her husband kneeling beside her, his attention focused entirely on her belly.

He caught her eyes, saying, "You are awake."

She smiled, yawning into her open palm. "I am enjoying the sun. I feel much too lazy to do anything more than lounge around."

Darcy rose from his knees to sit on a nearby chair. He took her hand, holding it within his. They were silent for a long moment, enjoying their own company accompanied by peace and quiet, admiring the view of the lake and hills spread in front of them.

"Do you know what day it is today?" Darcy asked.

"Monday," she answered, her head lolling to the side.

"The twentieth of September."

"And?"

He chuckled. "And I heard that women, not men, were sentimental, always remembering the anniversaries."

She frowned, concentrating. "September the twentieth," she repeated. "Help me. I do not remember."

"This day last year I asked you about your opinion of me and your feelings towards me."

"Ah, yes, of course!" She laughed. "The anniversary of our engagement. This baby makes me forget everything."

Darcy leaned forward, placing his cheek against the top of her belly. "Do you hear, my child? I proposed to your Mama exactly a year ago, and this time she accepted me. I was mighty proud of myself that day. She did not make it easy for me for the next three months, tempting me daily to misbehave myself. It was a sweet torture, though."

Elizabeth combed her fingers through his dark locks, a caress which he especially enjoyed, as a smile played on her lips. Suddenly the smile disappeared from her face and a frown marked her countenance. She shifted in place, moving her hand from her husband's head to the side of her stomach. Darcy did not notice anything and kept talking to the baby.

"Fitzwilliam, I daresay that the twentieth of September will mark yet another anniversary in our lives."

He looked up at her. "Why?"

"Because I think that the baby is coming."

His face went pale. "What?"

"The baby is coming now," she repeated.

Slowly, Darcy rose to his feet, his eyes focused on the wet spot at the front of her dress below her extended belly.

"Will you help me to my room?" she asked. "I need to change."

In response Darcy stared at her, perfectly immobilised.

She lifted her hand in his direction. "Fitzwilliam, will you help me, please?"

Finally he moved. With great care he helped her to her feet. Slowly they walked inside the house.

"Do you think that our child will be born today?" he enquired, his strong arm supporting her back.

"Or tomorrow," she breathed out.

"Better today."

"Why?"

"It is a good birthday, the twentieth of September."

"I will do what I can," Elizabeth murmured dryly, feeling the tightening in her stomach growing stronger and sharper with every second.

***

Thomas George Darcy did not grant his father's wish, and was born close to three in the morning on the twenty-first of September. Elizabeth insisted that the boy had a mind of his own, and in the future it proved to be a good description of his character. Darcy was deeply grateful to the Lord for the safe delivery of his firstborn as well as his wife's quick return to health.

Little Thomas thrived under the loving care of his parents and aunt Georgiana as well as the entire staff at Pemberley. The many relatives came to admire him, including his grandparents and aunts from Hertfordshire as well as the Earl of Matlock, who had himself become a proud grandfather to a fine boy earlier this year. Only Lady Catherine de Bourgh refused to acknowledge the happy news, ignoring the letter Darcy sent to her.

With the end of the year sad news came from Rosings Park, forcing Lady Catherine to search for a new parson. Mr. Collins died unexpectedly while working in his garden. His wife was relieved to hear from the physician that he did not suffer much.

Mrs. Collins decided to return to Hertfordshire. Her son, William Richard, which she called Richie, was now the sole heir to Longbourn. But as Mr. Bennet was in excellent health, Charlotte was welcomed back into her parents' home with open arms. Lady Lucas and Sir William enjoyed having their grandchildren under their roof very much indeed, especially little Lizzy, as she was a bright and engaging child.

Rather surprising was the fact that Colonel Fitzwilliam arrived with a visit to Netherfield even though Jane and Bingley were in the process of terminating the lease and moving up north. He stayed for longer than anyone expected, accepting Mrs. Bennet's invitation to Longbourn. He lived there for nearly two months before his duties called him back to his regiment. From her mother and Jane's letters, Elizabeth could safely assume that Colonel Fitzwilliam was discreetly courting Mrs. Collins, paying regular visits at Lucas Lodge, never forgetting to bring a gift to little Lizzie and Richie. Darcy thought that his cousin was biding his time, waiting with the official proposal for propriety reasons only because of the required mourning period.

As for Caroline Bingley, she never again tried to visit Pemberley or come close to Darcy, Elizabeth or Georgiana. The Darcys were invited to her wedding to a gentleman from Ireland, but they made their excuses and were absent at the ceremony. In her conversation with Elizabeth, Jane insisted that Caroline changed much and for the better. However, Elizabeth was not in the least interested in requiting their acquaintance. She liked to paraphrase her husband, saying that her good opinion, once lost, was lost forever.

The End.

4977645R00165

Printed in Germany
by Amazon Distribution
GmbH, Leipzig